MIDLIFE MOJO

Not Too Late Series, Book 3

by Victoria Danann

D1607582

HALLOW HILL

AT YULE

PROLOGUE

I WAS SURE I would never again experience anything more wonderful than Yule in Hallow Hill. It turns out the ancient pagans and Druids of the British Isles adopted the traditions of greenery, red ribbons and ornaments, and an attitude of you-can't-have-too-many-candles from the fae. Of course, in modern times humans substitute electric lights for candles, partly because it's convenient and pretty in its own way and, partly, because fae can control things like fire. We can't. They can also cause fully grown evergreen trees to appear, rooted to whatever spot they choose. Again, we go for a cut tree or a faux tree.

Hallow Hill spares no expense when it comes to celebrating seasonal milestones. Overnight, literally, multitudes of little twinkling lights lent the community the luster of midday. Storefronts and houses were decked with boughs of holly, grapevine, magnolia leaves (now that's magic), and so many pine branches that the entire village was fragrant.

It's magic that defies description.

That doesn't mean my life is problem free.

MY FULLY HUMAN, fully clueless daughter's college break will dovetail the Solstice Court Meet. I don't mean clueless in the sense of dumb. Quite the opposite. Evie may be one of the smartest cookies on the orb. I mean she thinks I'm a mild-mannered shopkeeper in a sleepy little English village. Only three words in that sentence can claim kin to reality; little English village. When it comes to what I'm really up to, she's ignorant as the day she was born.

AND I WANT to keep it that way.

IF ALL GOES well, I'll be out of magistrate robes in time to meet the plane and residents of Hallow Hill will behave themselves long enough for her to head back to the states thinking I live in a pretty little English village with nice, but possibly quirky neighbors.

OF COURSE, THAT'S not all. I also have a psychotic kelpie on the loose, intent on taking me for a one-way ride. That's not the reason why I'm stalling making a formal commitment to Keir, who has his heart set on a spring handfasting. I don't know why I'm hesitating. After all, he's everything a woman could want and way more.

My chief distraction is finalizing the docket for Solstice Court with a lot more insight now that I've survived my first court meet.

I'M SURE YOU want to know how things turned out with the young and amoral, power hungry Irish fae prince, Niall, and his gorgeous older brother, Diarmuid. Well, after a conversation with Queen Enya of the Scotia fae, who more or less owed me a favor, I made Niall her ward for a year and a day. During that time, Enya's brethren, a hale and hardy bunch of wildhaired Scots, will show Niall the meaning of tough love. One might argue that they're an odd choice for role models, but my intuition told me that, if there was a kernel of redemptive quality in Niall, the Scots would find it and try to smelt it into something worthwhile.

At the very least, a year's loss of freedom could only do him good.

The fact that neither Maeve nor Diarmuid objected to my ruling, in any way, tells its own story. Perhaps they're hoping for something like Scotia fae bootcamp and the miraculous return of a kid who doesn't embarrass his presitigious family. I'm mildly optimistic. Mildly because I fear Niall had the sort of psyche that won't be easily untwisted.

CHAPTER ONE

Jersey Devil, Part Deux

KEIR WASN'T THE sort to move around the house in silence. When he was up and about, I knew it. Unless I'd ended the night before with too much Bailey's.

As one of the dual natured, he might've had some noiseless cat traits, but in human form he was as rambunctious as a teenage jock.

Do not misconstrue this as complaining, even though that's how it sounds. I was eager for his company and not just for the usual reasons. I needed his help to make sense of the previous night's strange occurrence.

I was sitting by the kitchen fire with my laptop and a cup of ginger tea, still in my pretty pink and gray silky pajamas, when he appeared wearing nothing but draw-string pants.

The looked scrumptious as could be with his towel-dried mane of tawny hair, and I knew that, if I planted my face in his abs, I'd be treated to the heady scent of sephalian freshly washed with sheep's wool soap. Locally milled, of course.

He saw that my eyes were fixed on his midsection. After glancing down, his mouth formed one of my favorite expressions, the sexy, cocky smirk. Those pants had a way of accentuating his happy trail so that it drew the eye like a neon arrow.

"Like something you see?"

My moment of being transfixed was broken by his teasing. "I guess by now you'd know I was lying if I said no. So. Yeah. I like what I see."

His smile faded. "But something's wrong."

He looked around like he thought it might be something external. His eyes landed on the large pink crystal sitting on the table in front of me then shifted to the screen on my laptop. I had just typed my email password and the "SHOW" feature was turned on. It wouldn't have made any difference if he was human, but Keir's eyesight was phenomenal. He had no trouble reading an eight-point font from across a room.

"Mojomom?" It was a goodnatured heckle, but I wasn't feeling goodnatured.

"Stop reading my screen. You're invading my privacy." He waited. "And what's wrong with 'Mojomom'?"

"Nothing at all. I just don't usually think of you as a mum. I know you have offspring and all…"

"I don't have offspring. I have one, um, spring." It was just about then that I recognized I was blithering. Again. "Just one daughter." I trailed off.

He shook his head like he thought I'd been into the magic mushrooms. "Rita. Your password is up to you. I think it's cute."

"Damn right!"

He turned slowly and repeated his question with a firmness that wasn't there before. "What. Is. Wrong?"

I slumped and sighed. "Grab a spot of tea. I have a story to tell."

"Is it a good story?"

"I'll let you decide. After you hear it." With an enigmatic departing look he headed toward the kettle on bare feet that were unjustly beautiful on a male; perfectly formed minus the myriad flaws that're customary with feet. "Aren't you cold?"

His back was to me, but I plainly heard the chuckle. "I don't get cold, love."

"Then why are you such a good snuggler at night?"

With steaming cup in hand, he joined me by the fire. Not, apparently, because he craved the warmth.

"I wouldn't think of myself as proficient at snuggling in general. I snuggle with you because I like it. Not because I need it. And, if you think I'm good at it, eye of the beholder and all that."

"Huh."

He smiled into his cup just before blowing across the hot liquid, took a sip, then said, "But the pleasure of it is something we share in common."

An involuntary sigh erupted making me sound more vulnerable than I'd ever intended to be. Again. In the beginning there'd been a brief time when Cole looked at me adoringly and said lovely things.

"Storytime?" he prompted, seeing that I'd been carried into a reverie.

I recounted the entire story. How I'd awakened, gone

to the kitchen and had a conversation with a monstrous thing that claimed to be a Jersey Devil, by all the gods, had a pronounced Jersey accent.

"You know, if you said 'Jersey Devil' to anybody who's not me they'd say that's a hockey player." With a slight shudder, I added, "I kind of wish that's what I still thought, too. Anyhow, I woke up early and assumed it'd been an unusually vivid dream. But when I arrived in the kitchen, the rock that 'tells the future of virgins' was sitting on the island just as it had been in my, um…"

"Recollection?" he offered, when it was clear I was stumped for an appropriate word.

"Yeah. My recollection." Keir stared into his teacup. "Come on. Of the two of us, you're the one with nine hundred plus years of magic kind experience. Give."

"I admit that, comparatively, I have more experience in matters of magic. But hard as it may be to believe, I'm not an authority on everything."

"Every woman in a relationship lives to hear those words."

"Funny."

"What's not funny is that this pretty pink crystal,

which may or may not have mystical power, was delivered to my kitchen while we *slept*." My gaze jerked to Keir. "How likely is it that you'd sleep through a break-in? I mean I could. Sure. But not you! For that matter, my house isn't supposed to let people… or creatures, in without my permission. Right?"

"Right."

"Well?"

"Well, what?"

I chuffed. "How. Did. This. Get. Here?"

"I don't know, but being out of sorts with me will not solve your mystery, will it?" At that moment Keir sounded irritatingly English. Or maybe I was just irritated. He rose, cup in hand. "I'm going to my room to see if there's some American football on."

"It's the middle of the night in the U.S."

"Reruns."

I let him walk out because I was behaving badly and didn't seem to be able to dial the bitchmeter back. The idea of monsters prowling around my house in the middle of the night was unsettling to the core, even if their purpose was to leave gifts and messages.

A pop of green wood sap brought my gaze to the dancing fire in my counter-height kitchen fireplace. The light reflected on the planes of the crystal was hypnotic.

"What are you really?" I whispered to the crystal. "And why are you here?"

Resolve didn't creep up. It hit me like a lightning bolt. I practically jumped out of the chair and raced to the bedroom. Without paying much attention to what I was grabbing, I pulled on jeans, comfy shoes, and a long sweater. I power-walked back to the kitchen, grabbed the virgin oracle, and left without telling Keir where I was going. If he'd found football, I'd probably be back before he knew I'd been gone.

I hoped Esmerelda would be in the shop early because, I realized, I didn't know where she lived. Of course, the village was small enough that I could probably stand on the green and yell her name until somebody told me where to find her, but that wouldn't be my first choice.

Luck was with me. The old iron latch on the shop door moved when I gripped the handle. I was probably too winded for someone who'd only jogged three blocks, but I decided to consider the implications of that later.

"Esmerelda," I called. "The door was unlocked. Please tell me you can give me five minutes."

She drifted in with a raised eyebrow. "I'm terribly busy," she said with a raised eyebrow. "And it's very early."

"Of course. I'd never want to take your schedule for granted, but I've experienced an inexplicable event. And the door was unlocked," I repeated.

I could tell by the instant change in her demeanor that she was interested, but she sounded terse anyway.

"Inexplicable to whom? *You?*" After a slight dramatic pause, she added. "Or *me*?"

"Well, that's why I'm here. You're the queen soothsaying. So nothing, no matter how strange, is beyond you."

Esme's self-satisfied smile told me she'd been flattered and placated enough to be primed to help.

"Very well. Would you like tea?"

"Just had some. It sloshed around on my jog over here."

"You ran?" Her eyebrow came back up.

"I'm not sure it qualified as 'running', but it was something more than walking."

"What is so urgent?" At that point her eyes found the

rock I was gripping and lingered there. She gestured toward the little table where we usually sat for tea and consultation in silent invitation. After we sat, she said, "Is that a gift for me?"

My gaze jerked to the pink crystal. Her question threw me off. Because even though I was the furthest thing from a geology buff or rock collector, my hand tightened around the show-and-tell I'd brought. It seemed I didn't like the idea of parting with it.

"Um. Well. While I would love to make you a gift of almost anything I have, that's not why I brought this."

"Very well. Why did you bring it?"

I spilled the entire story in three breaths, which meant I talked fast. For me.

"I understand that the assassin might warn you of the danger." She glanced away and pressed her lips together like she was perturbed. "Since Maeve and her lot didn't bother. My sense is that it was a courtesy call. Nice, really. The reason behind the gift is what's really interesting about this."

I was shaking my head. "Disagree on two counts. First, 'interesting' is too mild an expression for this event. I think scary or anxiety-ridden would be more appropriate descriptions. Second, it's not the gift that's the worry. It's that this self-confessed Devil was in my house. My house that has state-of-the-art fae security! And, even more worrisome. It didn't wake Keir!" I took a breath and blew it out. "Then there's the confusion about whether I was asleep or awake. I have a vivid memory of getting up, going to the kitchen, and talking to the monster. Calmly, if I do say so myself." I was rather proud of that. "I don't remember going back to bed, but when I woke up, I remembered the whole thing and it felt like it happened. In the flesh."

"Hmmm."

"If you don't have more to give me than that I may need whiskey instead of tea."

"I don't have whiskey."

"Literal much?"

"I'm not the one suggesting hard liquor before break-fast." Esme's brow formed the scowl that meant she was trying to decide if I'd asked a question that was rhetorical or one that required a response. "Never mind. Moving on to the chase. Did I get an in-person visit from that thing or not?"

My phone growled like the MGM lion. What could be a more perfect ringtone for Keir? And it had never failed to make me smile. Until now.

"Hello?"

"Where are you?"

"Esme's."

"You didn't say you were leaving."

"I thought you'd be occupied with sports-o-rama long enough that you'd never know I was gone."

"Well." Pause. "I do. Know you're gone."

"Okay."

"The crystal is gone as well."

"Yeah," I answered slowly. "I have it right here."

He sighed. "It's just that... Well, I wanted to be sure you're okay."

It occurred to me that I'd related a bizarre supernatural occurrence involving the misplacement of a physical item, perhaps a creature as well, then left without a word, note, or text. It might have been thoughtless of me.

"I didn't mean to worry you. It was thoughtless of me to disappear." I instantly regretted using the word disappear. Speaking it out loud sparked an unpleasant zinger of anxiety in my gut. "Right after Esme tells me what happened last night, I'll come home and make gingerbread pancakes."

"You know how to make pancakes?" He sounded surprised.

"Not like Olivia. But then *nobody* cooks like Olivia."

"Okay."

"Okay."

"Bye."

"Bye."

When I looked up, I saw that Esmerelda was smirking and I wanted to know why. "What's that about?"

"I was recalling the day we met when I predicted you'd find love? And you were quite adamant that I was wrong?"

"What makes you think I've found love?"

It was a silly thing to say and I'm sure I looked outrageously sheepish trying to make that question sound valid. Never one to indulge in meaningless repartee, Esme simply grunted.

"So, this is an I-told-you-so moment? Okay. Go ahead and gloat. You're the amazing Esmerelda and I might be in love." Esme started to say something else, but I cut her off. "That's the most you're going to get. Now. Back to my problem."

"What problem is that?"

I gaped. "The thing that showed up in my kitchen? And left this?"

Her eyes lowered to the pink crystal on the table between us before locking on mine again. "I've heard you, Rita. I'm simply confused as to why you see this as a problem."

I grunted as I slouched back in my chair. "This isn't a game, Esme."

"Good. Because I don't like games and don't have time for them."

"When you have a life span as limited as mine, we'll talk about your claim that your time is at a premium. Until then, you've got time."

She sniffed. "Rita. Did the creature you saw hurt you?"

"No."

"Did he threaten to hurt you?"

"Did he say he was on a mission to protect you from harm?"

"Well. Sort of."

"Do you think he left an artifact that's intended to harm you?"

I looked at the crystal again. "Not sure." She narrowed her eyes. "Okay. I don't get the feeling that there's anything bad attached."

"Therefore?" she said.

I inhaled deeply.

I exhaled deeply.

"So, you're saying that, if he didn't intend me harm, and left an object that appears to be harmless, why am I upset?"

"Excellent. You've resolved your own dilemma."

"No. I haven't."

My supernatural guide was showing signs of potential exasperation building. "Rita…"

"Esme. You're used to strange things in your life. Strike that! I mean to say my strange is your normal. You probably take such events in stride. Monster visiting your kitchen in the middle of the night? Yawn. What else is new?

"But to me, such an occurrence is disturbing. Deeply.

Especially the fact that I don't remember what happened between the conversation in the kitchen and waking up in my bed this morning."

"Perhaps the creature sparked a latent, forbidden fantasy in your subconscious mind. Perhaps you engaged in illicit interspecies intimacy of a wild and hairy nature then blocked it out because your conscious mind couldn't deal with the images, the sensations, or the fact that you were unfaithful to the sephalian."

My mouth was hanging open to the extent my jaw would allow.

"You. Did. Not. Just. Say. That." Her mouth spread into a triumphant smile as she nodded with the sort of gleam that spells mischief on any face of any species. "Tell me that didn't happen right now before I need an ambulance," I said, touching my chest and wondering if I was having heart palpitations.

She indulged in a few more seconds of sadistic fun before saying, "Very well. That did not happen."

"I came to you for answers and comfort, *friend.* Instead, I've been taken on a House of Horrors ride. Before breakfast!"

"Perhaps you should ask yourself if I'm the best person to seek out when you need comfort."

"Agreed. I *am* asking myself that and I'm hearing the answer loud and clear. What about answers?"

"You already know most of it. The creature dropped by to deliver a message. It wasn't intended as a threat. It was twofold. First, you're in danger. Second, he's taking care of it. The gift was a courtesy among magic kind. Many human cultures also ascribe to the belief that you should bring a gift when visiting."

I couldn't help but wonder if that was a pointed remark. I cocked my head. "Am I being rude when I come to see you without a gift?" She glanced away. "Please tell me. I'd certainly want to know if I'm a walking faux pas."

"I am not offended when you arrive without a gift."

"Well. That's a relief. I'd have to stock up because I come by pretty often."

"Yes."

"Yes? That didn't give me much reassurance that I'm always welcome."

"As we discussed earlier, perhaps I'm not the best resource when the goal is comfort. Or what was the other thing? Reassurance?"

"I'll take what I can get. Now that you're finished messing with me, what does the sooth say about my unexplained time between talking to the Devil and waking up?"

Her mouth twitched ever so slightly. "Rita. You really can be dense at times. You were asleep the whole night." I scowled, then reached up to spread my WTF lines between my brows smooth. "What are you doing?"

"Trying to preserve what illusion of youth is left to me."

"I have no idea what that means."

"That makes us even. I have no idea how I could have slept through this experience and end up with a honest-to-gods physical souvenir like this." I raised the crystal for effect just in case there was any chance she didn't know what I meant.

Calculating the odds of Esme being wrong, no matter how farfetched her explanation, I decided to surrender graciously. "How do you know?"

"You don't come here to find out *how* I know things. You come here to find out the things I know."

"Well, you've got me there. But if I dreamed it, what about this?"

I motioned toward the crystal.

"In your recollection of what transpired between the creature and yourself, do you recall accepting the gift?"

I thought back. "I said it was pretty. He said it tells the future of virgins. I said thank you."

"Sounds like acceptance to me."

"Yes, but I'm not used to things in my dreams sitting on my kitchen table, in pretty-as-you-please physical form, when I wake up." I knocked on wood. "And I say thank all that's holy for that. I'd like to keep it that way."

"Okay."

"What do you mean okay? How does a thing go from being part of a dream to being a real piece of object d'art? Or more. Who knows?"

"If you accepted a magical gift from magic kind on an astral plane, it will manifest in this reality. Simple as that."

"Well, for crying out loud, Esme. Why didn't you just say so in the first place?"

"Because I didn't fully grasp the depth of your ignorance."

With a slight shake of my head, I said, "I hate it when you insult me in a situation where I'm bound by manners to thank you anyway."

"If you really hated the double-bind situations you constantly create, you wouldn't do it."

"Oh. So now you're a shrink?" She rolled her eyes. "Thank you for your help."

"You're welcome. Come anytime I'm not busy and in the mood for company." She chuckled at that and disappeared into the rear of the shop.

"In other words, never?" I called. "Is that what you meant?"

Receiving no answer, I swiped up the crystal and speed-walked back to my house. The dogs were out with the puppies. I ran over and gave each one of the four the canoodling they deserved, noticing that my babies didn't like me to give their parents *too* much attention. They let me know by taking my hands gently between their jaws and pulling me away. I laughed at this latest comedy routine, feeling my good humor settle back into place where it was supposed to be constant. I half ran into my house as the door opened and closed for me.

"I'm home!" I yelled.

Keir arrived in the kitchen at the same time I did. "With a better outlook?" he asked.

"Yeah. Sorry I was grumpy earlier. I'll tell you about it over pancakes. Go watch people jump off cliffs into mud or whatever's on this morning." He snickered because I'd actually caught him doing just that; some weird contest in Russia or Monrovia or some other place where people obviously have too little to amuse themselves. I watched for three fascinated minutes before deciding I didn't want to know more. "I'll call when ready."

I got a smile and a brief nod before he returned to the sports lair. One of Keir's virtues that was especially near and dear to my heart was that he was easygoing, always quick to bounce back after I made a mess of household harmony.

Left standing in the kitchen alone, I had to wonder what I'd been thinking when I blurted out gingerbread pancakes. I hadn't made them since Evie was ten years old. I didn't know why I'd landed on that as a makeup gesture, but now I had to try to remember the recipe.

Forty-five minutes later Keir arrived at the kitchen

door.

"You are killing me with the smell of bacon and promise of gingerbread."

His eyes drifted toward the table as he spoke and back to me.

"We're ready," I said with a smile, scooping up two plates of pancakes with sides of bacon. A full pound for Keir.

He sat as I set the plates on the table. "I've never been fed by a mate before."

"Okaaaaay."

"It's… special."

"It certainly is. And let's keep it that way."

He chuckled because he knew it was pointless to think I'd cook often. Between the pub and Olivia, it was mostly covered.

Keir set to work covering his pancakes with enough syrup to give most humans a sugar seizure, then took a bite.

However, satisfying it was for him to be fed by me, I felt just that satisfied watching him swoon over my cooking. There was something primal about it and I suddenly wanted him for dessert.

"This is beyond good," he said. "I've never had gingerbread pancakes. How is it possible that I missed such a profound earthly delight?" I shrugged and smiled, loving the praise. "Can we have them every day?"

"Nice try. No. Once a year. If you're a good boy."

He put his fork down and gave me the look that said he knows where to find the bedroom. "I know how to be a good boy."

I laughed. "Yeah. You do."

CHAPTER TWO

Jinxed and Jilted

E ARLY DECEMBER WAS a joy. There was a constant smile on my face and a hum in my vocal cords as I'd occasionally remember a piece of a favorite holiday tune. The decorations and lights made all kinds of magical happy feelings.

Libations were available everywhere and offered often. I rarely said no. While I was experiencing enhanced health and longevity benefits, my nerve endings were still completely human. That had its upside when I was in bed with Keir. It had its downside when I was on the English moors in December.

You might ask why I'd be walking the moors in December? My puppies had taken the walk across the lane and moved in with me. Next to Keir, they were life's greatest pleasure. I laughed at their antics, was soothed by their precious snoring, and felt comforted by their need to give affection as well as receive it. Conversely, the wolf-dogs lived for their morning walk and I could not bring myself to deny them what they wanted most.

No kind of weather was a deterrent for them. Sometimes I thought they enjoyed their romp even more when it was miserable for me. They thrived on wet snow and brutal wind. Go figure.

Did I mention how fast they were growing?

Fast.

They were already in the awkward early-adolescent stage and were born comedians. I had to stop and bend over with laughter after watching Frey trot alongside Fen, keeping pace step for step, his ear firmly clamped between her teeth. He wore a look that plainly said, "What're you gonna do?"

There was no way of knowing how much my wolf dogs understood, but it seemed clear to me that they're pleased and content when I'm happy.

As Keir had predicted, they thought it was the most normal thing in the world to live with a shifter who could become a giant winged lion at will. Conversely, Keir didn't gush over my pups much, but he fed them as often as I did and, sometimes, I heard him talking to them when I was in another part of the house.

I couldn't believe it was already time to sort through briefs for the Solstice Court Meet docket. I found myself standing just inside the door of my study staring at the three piles Lochlan had dropped off. Olivia had started a cheery fire made even cheerier by the greenery and twinkle lights that draped the length of the mantle.

I was conflicted. I liked the work. I also liked the feeling of a heart full of good cheer because of the beauty of the season. And I knew that, once I opened those files, the lightheartedness of the season would be dampened.

The wolfdogs had padded in behind me and flopped down on my rug. For the first time it occurred to me that my pets didn't shed. Or smell. Or require any grooming upkeep at all. Huh. It occurred to me, as it did often, that I very well could be the luckiest woman alive.

Looking at the files again, I inhaled deeply. Frey whimpered slightly like she was in tune with my dilemma. At times I thought she was as intuitive as a sensitive person, and maybe she was.

"Yeah," I said to her. "Life is full of grownup choices. Time to come back to the real world."

A scoff forced its way out of my mouth when I replayed what I'd just said. It seemed that it hadn't taken long for me to think of my fantastical magic world duties as the 'real world'. Life is strange.

I looked up at the slight knock on my study door. Olivia had brought a painted wood tray with tea. It was a welcome sight.

"Thought you'd like a warmup, Magistrate. Your cheeks are still rosy from stomping around the moors with those beasts."

Both dogs looked up when hearing themselves called 'those beasts'.

"That's so thoughtful of you, Liv."

Honestly, how bad could things be if somebody else decorated my house for the holidays, started a fire in anticipation of me going to work, and brought me tea without being asked?

"Okay," she said as she set the tray down next to the pile of briefs. She'd said okay to me so often that she was getting close to the American pronunciation. "Shall I close the door?"

"No. The 'beasts' can come and go as they please."

She glanced their way, nodded, and withdrew without making a sound.

"Oh! Olivia?" She reappeared within seconds. "Are we hosting lunch today?"

"We are."

"What are we having?"

"Szechuan beef with leeks on brown rice. And carrot cake with almonds for dessert."

"I love your Szechuan beef."

She no longer blushed at compliments, but she did look demure. "I know."

"Who are we having?"

"Maggie, John David Weir, Lily, you, me, and the sephalian."

I noticed that Olivia never called Keir by his name. She always referred to him as the sephalian.

"Did we get some more of that white ale he likes?"

"Delivered last evening."

"Super good. Thank you."

Olivia had long since given up the curtsy that turned into a slight bow. Now she expressed deference and acquiescence by lowering her eyelids for a couple of seconds.

Left alone again, having used my last excuse to put off getting down to business, I switched on the twin library lamps and took a seat. By the time I heard people arriving for lunch, I was deep into the details of a case that had caught my interest.

A surviving Fear Laith, perhaps the only one in existence, had been turning up in local reports in the Scottish Highlands. The Bureau had filed an application for guardianship, suggesting that the increasingly choking encroachment of human population had left the creature nowhere to hide. The Bureau proposed relocating the creature within faerie, where he or she would be safe and pose no threat to the magic world's carefully guarded secrets.

A fae lord was irritated by a prophet's prediction that involved his fortunes and sued for recantation.

That was the first file of the maybe stack, meaning that Lochlan would determine if there was time to include it on this court meet's docket.

LUNCH WAS A nice break although I must admit that my thoughts kept drifting back to aspects of some of the briefs I'd scanned. As soon as the last guest departed, I resettled myself at my library table and pulled the next brief from the top of the pile closest to me.

A family member of the Irish fae House of Bayune had been boar hunting in Finland with his older brothers. He stopped to admire the magnificence of the scenery and, while separated from his family, was taken into faerie by a dalliance of snow sprites.

I have gathered that fae are particularly susceptible to falling in love at first sight and, the more I hear about the ramifications of that, the happier I am that it rarely happens to humans.

One of the Finnish snow sprites had seen the boy and told her sisters that she would surely die if she couldn't have him. Naturally, being fond of their sister and all, they conspired to help with the abduction. Political consequences didn't figure into their plan.

The kid, whose name was Caesperic, happened to be a

nephew of Maeve's. Maeve sent a respectful, politely worded missive to Queen Ilmr, ruler of the northern tribes, requesting that she intervene and gain Caesperic's release. Queen Ilmr replied that she magnanimously allowed Irish fae hunting privileges in Finland and had been glad to host them but would not use her office to intercede in matters of love.

When Maeve received and read the reply, the entirety of the Irish faerie mound shook like a Richter Scale level four earthquake. Her brother, the boy's father, was just as livid, but not powerful enough to cause worlds to tremble.

The pretty parchment caught fire when Maeve threw it up into the air and was burned to ash by the time it floated to the stone floor. In my head I could see the Irish queen stomping out of the room, demanding to know Diarmuid's whereabouts.

According to the summary in front of me, Maeve entreated Diarmuid to take up a Wild Hunt for the purpose of recovering Caesperic. Diarmuid not only recovered Caesperic, but snatched the lovelorn snow sprite, Eevi, as well.

When Queen Ilmr learned of this, she sent a missive to

Maeve demanding Eevi's return. When Maeve replied that she wouldn't use her office to intercede in matters of love, it was Ilmr's turn to pitch a regal fit.

Ilmr replied that it was not the same because her snow sprite would die in Ireland's mild climate.

Maeve ignored her.

Rather than acting on her impulse to harness up the royal reindeer and go to war with the Irish, Ilmr was persuaded by the curia regina to set a civilized example and employ legal channels first.

Shortly after I'd heard Olivia leave for the day, Keir appeared at my study door.

I looked up. "Have you ever been boar hunting in Finland?"

"Can't say that I have. I'm afraid my second nature might be overcome with excitment and facilitate the untimely extinction of a species."

I could feel the lines between my brows. "I didn't know that losing control of your second nature was a possibility."

He chuckled. "It's not. I'm joking. I don't have time for pissant royal pastimes like boar hunting." He rolled his eyes for good measure.

"That's right. There're far too many sports to be watched."

With a good-natured laugh, he got me back on topic. "Why did you ask? About boar hunting."

"It seems your mum is often in the middle of things."

He sighed, shoved both hands in his pockets, and leaned against the door jamb. "What's she done now?"

"Threatened to start a war with the Finnish fae."

"Good gods. What over?"

"Do you know a kid named Caesperic?"

Keir's eyes cast about for a couple of seconds like he was thinking it over. "Cousin?"

"Nephew."

Keir nodded. I gave him the Cliff's Notes version of the abduction and recovery that was coupled with another abduction.

"So, is that case making it to the Yuletide docket?"

My sarcastic snort said it all, but I added words anyway. "Cases that involve staving off wars always make the docket. It's a rule." I glanced back at the file. "I guess I should dig into this Wild Hunt thing and learn more about it. References keep coming up. The strange thing is that I get the sense that I've read about it, but don't remember what I read."

"Um-hum."

My head jerked toward where he stood. "You know something?"

"Well. There are fafgaleons of protections built into the Hunts to make sure they're disguised. It's not something fae want to share with humans."

"What kind of protections?" I scowled again. "You mean fuzzy memory kinds of protections?"

"It's a possibility."

"Well, that won't do. I'll take it up with Lochlan. Exceptions need to be made in my case so that I'm not protected from knowledge of the Hunt or the Hunt isn't protected from me, whichever may be the case."

"So happens I agree."

"Now what was it I can do for you?"

"I'm going to run over and look in on Tregeagle before lunch. Make sure everything is good."

"You want to take Romeo?"

He grinned. "Does the sun rise in the east?"

"No. The earth spins eastward making it seem to primitives that the sun is rising in the east."

"I'm a poet. Don't confuse me with science."

My eyes widened. "You're a poet?" I shook my head and laughed softly. "Whatever you say. See you for dinner."

"Indeed, you will."

The sound of his footsteps receded as he went deeper into the house. I heard the faint sound of Romeo's door opening followed by the rumbling purr of his hoity toity engine and knew that sephalian and talking car were about to have a mutually satisfying outing. No doubt one that would be hair-raising for most of us.

I twisted in my chair so that I could consciously appreciate the moment. It was unusual to be in the house by myself. While I loved the liveliness of the household, I also cherished an occasional silence. It seemed to bring forward into awareness the crackle, pop, and hiss of green wood on the fire, Fen's soft snoring, and the deeply satisfying energy of contentment. I exhaled a deep breath filled with gratitude and smiled when Frey raised her head and looked at me.

After thoroughly absorbing the moment, I shuffled toward the kitchen in my moose slippers, the ones with the big crossed eyes, fuzzy antlers, and red nose to make my own mug of cocoa. I'd found that the act of occasionally doing things for myself was its own pleasure, a reminder that I still knew how coupled with a physical task of self-nurture.

Life was good.

The dogs were by the fire where I'd left them when I returned with my "gourmet" hot chocolate. I poked at the fire, not because it needed to be done, but because I liked doing it, and settled at my table with the next brief from the pile.

A young Deutsch nobleman had been jilted by a French princess he'd been courting. When the relationship ripened to a stage upon which he became insistent about lovemaking, she broke things off. He responded by stealing her most treasured possession and the reason for the young woman's refusal. A unicorn. She knew that the cost of surrendering her virginity would mean giving up communion with the unicorn. Because, as everybody knows, unicorns will only tolerate the company of virgins.

I couldn't help but look over at the pink rock, which I'd set on my library table. Whenever the crystal sat in the same room as a fire, the dance of flames always found the crystalline planes and reflected the movement making it seem alive. Without thought I reached over to touch it. As I ran my hand down one of the smooth angles the fire touched a drop of sap and made a loud pop. I startled, then laughed at myself.

Frey raised her head to see what she was missing, decided that her human was nuts, and promptly returned to the more serious pastime of magical canine napping.

I returned to reading. Apparently, the entirety of faerie was mad at the Deutschman about the theft because unicorns were rare and sacred to the lot of them. So, the suit was being brought jointly by the French princess, her family, and the Bureau of Behavioral Oversight. They wanted their unicorn back and, well, who could blame them for that?

I set the case on the yes pile thinking the Deutschman must have been delirious to think he'd get away with stealing somebody's unicorn. Even the wording of that is tricky because I gathered that unicorns can't belong to a person. They can choose to keep company for a time. That, of course, raised the question of how the Deutsch nobleman, Balder, which I personally thought was an unfortunate name, was able to hold the unicorn against its will.

Feeling satisfied with my day's work I was thinking about a hot bath. I glanced toward the window and registered two things.

First, it was snow time. Snow wasn't common in that part of England and even less likely in mid-December, but every afternoon big fluffy flakes fell for just long enough to keep the village looking pretty as a snow globe. Magic definitely has its perks.

Second, Lochlan was returning home. I tugged on my big snuggly windowpane turtleneck that was lying across the leather chair as I hurried for the front door.

"Lochlan!" I called just as he was closing his door.

There's something so comforting about knowing people with consistent temperaments. I would never have to wonder if Lochlan would greet me with a happy smile. I knew he would.

"Magistrate!" he said as if it was a family reunion and

we hadn't seen each other for years. He looked down at my moose slippers as I trudged forward in the new snow.

"Oh gosh. These aren't made for snow are they? Can you come over for a minute?"

"Certainly." He closed his door and followed.

Inside my house I withdrew feet from damp house shoes. "Let me grab other shoes. Wait anywhere. Do you want tea? Or anything?"

"No," he said as he withdrew a pocket watch from his vest pocket like a character from a Victorian movie. "I believe Ivy has plans for pot and pastry."

"I won't keep you. Be right back."

I grabbed big thick socks, pulled them on, and hurried back to the living room not wanting to be the cause of keeping Ivy waiting.

"One of the cases indirectly involved the Wild Hunt."

"Yes?"

"I don't seem to be able to get a grasp of what it is and how it's, um, conducted. I have a vague notion that I've read about it, maybe more than once. Could it be that I have and don't remember? Keir said he thought there might be protections."

Lochlan's high beam smile had disappeared and he looked serious. "Decent probability that. And, if true, it's something that needs correcting. Especially if there's a case involving the Hunt." I nodded. "We'll have to get a special dispensation to make an exception for you."

"You mean this isn't something that normally goes along with being magistrate?"

"No." He shook his head. "Nothing automatic. It's an item that requires presentation of cause. That's certainly present here. I'll contact the authorities."

That stopped my thought processes dead. "The authorities?" I said slowly. "What does that mean? Who are they? What are they? And why am I just now hearing about something called 'the authorities'?"

"Oh." He waved it off. "It's not as official as I made it sound. It's a trio of charmed ones who make sure that the most delicate matters of magic kind are veiled from human knowledge."

"Charmed ones," I said drily.

"I don't want to keep you from tea with your wife, but I *will* be wanting to hear more about this."

He nodded. "Of course."

VICTORIA DANANN

"How soon do you think you can get protections lifted for me? Special dispensation, did you say?"

"Soon. Perhaps tomorrow."

"Okay. Thanks for stopping. Tell Ivy I said hi. And Happy Yule."

His smile returned. "Happy Yule."

A HOT SOAK in my dream bath never failed to make me feel pampered. That dip was no exception, but it was somewhat less relaxing because I was preoccupied with thoughts about the Wild Hunt. I supposed learning that it was knowledge forbidden to humans made it all the more intriguing because... I almost laughed out loud. Human nature.

I was pulling on fresh French terry pants when I heard Romeo's door. A couple of minutes later, I saw Keir's opaque image through the fogged over mirror in in front of me.

"You don't look ready to go to pub," he said.

"How'd you find things?"

"All's well." He dipped his chin. "But I have news."

I wiped a swath of steam away from the glass then

gathered by the sparkle I saw in his eyes that it was juicy.

"You have the look of gossip. Really good gossip," I added.

"That's because it is," he teased.

"What do you know? Spill. I hate manufactured dramatic tension."

He chuckled as he leaned his back against the door. "You know that tempts me to want to drag this out. I'm very partial to watching you squirm." He wiggled his eyebrows.

I let out a half-shout of exasperation. "You lummox!"

He lowered his chin. "I love it when you talk dirty."

"I'M NOT TALKING DIRTY! I'M *INSULTING* YOU!" He laughed. "Fine. I'll go ask Lochlan." I moved toward the closet to get thick socks and shoes that would withstand snow. And clothes to go with them, of course.

Keir just looked at his nails. "Okay. But I doubt that he knows yet. You could say it's breaking news. Too soon to have gotten round."

"Molly?" He shook his head. "Maggie?"

"Too early. She'll undoubtedly hear later if she has errands tonight."

By that he meant if she'd be called upon to wail an approaching death here or there.

Deciding to change tactics, I tried pleading with puppy dog eyes. Bingo. I could see the second he caved. "Great Paddy's piddle," he said under his breath. "You win. Are you ready for this?"

"TELL ME ALREADY!" I was shamelessly breathless.

"Keep your pants on." His eyes traveled downward. "On second thought…"

"KEIR!"

His chuckle told me he was having way too much fun torturing me by withholding info.

"Very well, Magistrate. Rumor has it that Maeve is stepping aside, giving her crown over to Diarmuid."

I frowned, not sure that was welcome news. Dealing with Maeve could be tricky. She was powerful, petulant and seemed to have an unhealthy fixation on Keir; meaning that she might be a touch jealous of moi. If I was right about that, it was a little messed up. Like a reverse Oedipal complex. But that aside, I'd encountered Diarmuid in my first court meet and knew him to be every bit as arrogant as one would expect of Maeve's fair-haired and favorite heir.

"It's a political bombshell."

"Well put. Let's go to dinner."

"I thought we'd stay in tonight. As it turns out, that might be just as well. Since you'll be conveying all the ins and outs of the 'breaking news'."

"Staying in? Am I cooking?"

I chuckled. "We could toss a coin. Or I could make grilled cheese sandwiches. And heat up tomato soup."

"Yes to grilled cheese. No to tomato soup."

"Just as well. You can't have it if you can't say it."

"There's nothing wrong with the way I say tomato. Americans didn't invent the word, you know. There's a valid reason why the language is called *English*."

I mulled that over long enough to know when I'd been bested. There was no worthy argument. So, I let it go with a shrug and a sigh.

"I saw your wet moose slippers by the front door. I guess you discovered they're not snowshoes?" he asked.

Caught.

"I noticed Lochlan coming home, ran out to catch him, and, well, yeah, you saw the result. He agrees that I need to have the brain fog lifted so I can understand the Wild Hunt."

"I'd tell you, but at present I suppose it would bypass your conscious mind."

I finished towel drying my hair, stabbed at it with fingers until it looked as wild as the eighties, and turned to face him. "Well, now we have to establish that there's something I know that you don't. To re-establish the balance."

"What do you know that I don't?"

"If I told you, then you'd know, too."

He reached out and pulled me toward his body by catching hold of the little silk tie at my waist.

"Perhaps you could *show* me."

"Perhaps I…" He smothered the rest of that sentence with a kiss.

My body was primed to be welcoming of his intentions by being warm, clean, and relaxed. I pulled back and said, "What will you have, sir? Dinner or delight?" He grunted. "Never mind. Here's a proposal. I'll make dinner. You feed the dogs. Then you'll tell me what this change of regime means to me personally and professionally."

Realizing how that sounded, I added, "Not that it's all about me."

"Of course not," he deadpanned.

"Then we'll make it an early night."

His responding grin said he wholeheartedly approved of the plan.

I stopped at the door and turned around, "Have you, um, been on one of these Wild Hunt things?"

He nodded. "I have."

"Is it fun?"

His face went through a series of expressions, some almost contorted. I'd never seen him have trouble deciding what to say to me.

"Gosh. If it's that hard to figure out whether it's fun or not, I'm got to go with not."

"It's just that, if I say yes, and you disapprove when you have full knowledge, I don't want you to think…"

"You're afraid I'll judge you?"

"Are you being funny?"

I shook my head. "For once, no."

"Then the answer is yes. I suppose I'm concerned that you'll like me less."

"Ridiculous."

"No. It's not. You have perspectives about various things that are quite different from those of magic kind."

"Well, I like you just fine right now. So, let's not borrow trouble."

After a brief pause, he said, "Brilliant," in a decisive way, as if that concluded the matter. "I'll have six."

"Six what?"

"Grilled cheese sandwiches."

One of the things I've learned is that magic kind are not big on conversational segues. They see no reason to ease into a change of topic.

"You're bragging," I replied. "Nobody, not even you, can eat six grilled cheese sandwiches."

"Is that a dare?"

I laughed. "No. It's not. You can have seven if you want."

He seemed to be thinking it over. "I could eat seven, but then I'd probably go to sleep and the after-dinner portion of the evening's entertainment would suffer because of my lack of consciousness."

"Golly. Maybe you *are* a poet."

With an almost-inaudible snicker he turned toward the mudroom to feed the dogs. That was my cue to pull ingredients out of my restaurant-grade refrigeration column and an iron skillet out of the cabinet for use as a griddle.

When Keir was finished feeding the dogs and returned to the kitchen, I was still standing with the refrigerator door open.

"What are you doing, love?" he asked.

"Staring at the Kerrygold pure Irish butter blocks."

"Why?"

"I can't decide whether to use the silver, which is un-salted, or the gold, which is salted. Do you have a preference?"

"Here. Let me." Keir closed the refrigerator then gently guided me toward one of the Hemingway barstools and encouraged me to sit. I did. He then reached for one of Olivia's plain black aprons, which I thought looked scrumptious on him, and grabbed the silver, unsalted butter.

It didn't escape my notice that I'd spent decades being the caregiver to a husband and daughter who didn't reciprocate. It wasn't just that they didn't do things for me. I was inclined to believe that neither of them gave much thought as to whether I also needed kindness, comfort, nurture, or any sort of reassurance that I was loved. Loved more than if I'd been hired domestic help.

Lately, since I'd moved to Hallow Hill, Evie had begun to show signs of maturity in the sense that she seemed interested in me and my well-being. Someday the relationship might gradually turn into primal connection plus friendship. That would be nice.

In any case, Keir's demonstrations of affection through acts of service warmed my heart all the way down to my belly button.

"I really do know how to make grilled cheese sandwiches," I said lamely.

"No one questions that, love."

I looked at the fireplace and said, "Light." The house, understanding my desire, which would have to be called very cool in anybody's book, caused a flame to jump to life under the fire Olivia had set. Within seconds that was followed by the little 'poof' of perfectly arranged tinder catching all at once.

Looking back at Keir's operation, I said, "You're using yellow *and* white cheese?"

"I thought I would. Is that alright with you?"

"That... sounds amazing. Now I'm *really* glad you're the one making dinner."

He smiled as he shook his head slightly and reached into the refrigerator to get a glass jar of Molly's tomato soup. I liked it so much, especially on cold days, that Olivia kept it stocked in my refrigerator. Sometimes instead of tea, I'd have a cup of pub made fresh tomato soup. Good no matter how you pronounce it. Sometimes, if I was hungry, I'd add a little cream and turn it into tomato bisque.

Keir poured half the jar's contents into a saucepan and set it on the stove atop the modest gas flame that fanned out when he turned the dial.

Stretching my neck upward to oversee what he was doing, I said, "That doesn't look like enough for both of us."

"It's not," he said. "This is just for me. If you want some, get your own."

I laughed. "I have questions."

"Hmmm?"

"About the thing."

"If it's about the butter, the reason why I chose unsalt-ed is because…"

"Don't be a smart aleck. It's not about the butter. It's about the Diarmuid thing and you know it."

Fen and Frey came running in, tails wagging. They'd eaten, gone outside, and come to the kitchen to shake snow off their coats. As snowflakes were thrown off by the violence of coat-shaking, they became big droplets of water in the warm air, landing on me, and everything else around.

"Arghhhhh! Dogs!" I intended to be cross with them but ended up laughing instead. "Go to the mudroom."

I don't know what part of that sentence had become the signal command they understood, but they'd come to know what it meant. They raced off to the mudroom to wait for me to drag big towels out of the overhead cabinet and dry them off. They loved it and I suppose they thought it was a game. Certainly, since someone else fed them that night, drying them off and giving them some attention was the least I could do.

When I appeared back in the kitchen, I said, "Is something wrong with the weather?"

Keir looked away from the skillet long enough to ask, "What do you mean?"

"The dogs were wearing fresh snow."

"Why does that mean there's something wrong with the weather?"

"Because it snows in the afternoon. Not at night."

He turned to flip sandwiches before finally saying, "I don't think it's a rule."

"Okay. I'll be back. I'm going to put on dry clothes."

"Hustle. Grilled cheese is only good right off the griddle."

"Yes, boss."

I threw the dog-spray clothes on the bathroom floor and shimmied into fresh 'at leisure' or 'at home' or whatever may be the current term for I-don't-care-I-want-to-be-comfortable clothes.

On my way back to the kitchen I heard…

Don't turn around, oh oh

(Ja, ja)

VICTORIA DANANN

Der Kommissar's in town, whoa oh

I opened the door without looking to see who was there. After all, I had two wolfdogs, a sephalian, a magical house, and possibly a car to protect me.

Maggie stood on the porch wearing a clover green wool coat topped with a tartan shawl, looking pretty with snowflakes in hair that was a mix of white and fading auburn.

"Maggie," I said.

"Have ye heard?" She sounded like she might've run the full sixteenth of a mile to my house.

"Heard?"

"About Diarmuid?"

I opened the door wider and pulled her in. "Not the whole story. Keir was just about to fill in details. Come in and take off your coat. We're having grilled cheese and tomato soup. Sound good?"

She looked toward the kitchen. "Well. Do no' mind if I do. We had tourists throughout the day. I worked right through, I did."

"Well. Let's get you fed then." I closed the door.

"Keir!" I called. "We need more tomato soup. Maggie's staying for supper."

Maggie turned to head toward the kitchen.

Don't turn around, oh oh.

Ignoring the musical instruction, I turned around and opened the door before more could be sung.

"Lochlan. Hi."

"Good evening, Magistrate. Heard some interesting news. So, I hurried right over."

"Sure. Come in. Where's Ivy?"

"She and her sisters are doing something or other with mandrake plants tonight." He shrugged. "Girls only."

"Well then. Come have dinner with us. It's simple fare but Keir knows his way around a spatula."

"If you're certain it's not an imposition."

"Nothing of the kind," I assured him and meant it.

I didn't know how the extent of our ability to churn out grilled cheese sandwiches, but assumed it was limited. Keir might have to eat four instead of six and supplement his epic appetite with something else. I was pretty sure there was a berry pie in the freezer column.

As we approached the kitchen, I could hear Maggie talking to Keir.

"Stop right there," I said. "Say nothing more if I'm not in the room. I don't want to miss anything." Turning to Lochlan, "You're welcome to hang your jacket on the cloak hooks in the mudroom." To Keir I said, "Four for dinner."

We exchanged a look, but neither of our guests noticed.

I set the table for four while Keir opened the refrigerator. After looking inside for a minute, he said, "Perhaps a salad would complement the evening's fare?"

"What a wonderful thought!" I agreed.

FIFTEEN MINUTES LATER the four of us sat down to a humble but satisfying supper.

"So, who wants to go first?" I asked. Lochlan, Maggie, and Keir all began talking at the same time. I held up a hand. "Want to draw straws?" When no response was forthcoming, I said, "Keir and I had already begun a conversation. I gather on the same topic. So, please," I looked at him across the table, "continue. Tell me what's happened and why it's causing such a stir. Don't make any assumptions about my understanding of this event. Treat me like a child."

Both our guests looked toward Keir, who took the task every bit as seriously as I'd come to expect. He proved that by opening with, "Go to your room. The adults are talking."

"Ha. Ha. More precisely then. Treat me like a human."

"Very well. As I said earlier, I have it on loose authority that Maeve is passing ye olde sceptre to Diarmuid." Maggie and Lochlan both nodded. "So far as why that's causing a stir? If true, that will make him the most powerful figure in faerie." He decided to clarify further, no doubt for my benefit. "In all of magic kind really. Since he was already leader of the Wild Hunt, he'd become the Di Anu, the masculine embodiment of Irish faerie. More than king. God, almost."

Lochlan and Maggie both looked at me, possibly for a reaction. "Would he still be subject to decisions made by the court?" When no one answered, I began to feel anxious. "You don't know? Or you don't want to tell me."

Lochlan cleared his throat. "The last time there was a

living Di Anu was before Merle the Mathemagician's grand experiment. It's a question that hasn't been answered because it hasn't come up."

"Are you saying that he could also be the embodiment of anarchy? Not accountable to anyone in any way?"

Keir took a deep breath.

Lochlan swallowed the bite of sandwich in his mouth and said, "That is one possibility. We need to proceed carefully and diplomatically."

"I'll be tellin' ye this though," Maggie put in. "Of the lot of them, Diarmuid's my pick for likeliest to be seein' reason."

I looked at Keir. "You're an insider. Do you concur with Maggie?"

Sitting back with arms folded over his torso, Keir said, "I'm not as much an insider as you might think. But I agree he's the most levelheaded in the family."

"Pass the soup," Lochlan said.

Since our original plans had expanded to included company for dinner, Keir had heated up all the tomato soup in the refrigerator and transferred it to a Jan Barboglio tureen. Jan Barboglio might seem out of place in

Hallow Hill to some, but it worked for me.

"You started by saying it's a rumor. Has it been confirmed?" I was looking at Keir, but would've accepted an answer from anybody qualified to say.

That was Lochlan. "No *formal* announcement as of yet, but our sources are reliable."

"What else?" My question was answered by silence. "Well, I guess it's a good thing the kelpie snafu was decided before this, huh?"

Lochlan looked thoughtful. "I don't see Diarmuid being the sort to choose to undermine the underpinnings of a system that's working. I suspect the case involving his brother would go much the same. Not a lot of love lost there."

"He represented Niall in court," I said. "Even mounted a farfetched defense about kelpies being the same as domesticated horses. As I remember, it seemed like he was playing to the crowd; what Americans would call grandstanding."

"Well, that's just it, isn't it?" Keir said. "It *was* farfetched. Everybody who was present knew it. He was basically paying lip service to having his clan's back, while at the same time manipulating the outcome he ultimately wanted. Which was to free the kelpies and put the incident behind the house of Bayune."

I stared at Keir for a few beats. "You're saying he's the most dangerous sort of political operative. Machiavellian."

Keir pursed his lips before saying, "Cunning and manipulative like Machiavelli? Could be. Unscrupulous? Remains to be seen. This is not necessarily bad news. He might be a better ruler than Maeve."

"Yes," Lochlan agreed, nodding his head. "He's been touched by the hand of fate. No doubt about it."

"Before today I didn't even know a kingship was on the table. I mean all the current rulers are queens, right?" I asked Lochlan.

"Indeed, queens are traditionally heads of state because they're the creative arm of faerie. In essence, what's more divine than creativity? Nothing. That's how all religious stories begin. With an introduction to the all-powerful describing how he or she created the world."

"The queens create the faerie mounds," I said, "but don't call themselves gods."

"Exactly so," Maggie jumped in. "We would no' stand

for that kind of…"

"Hubris?" Lochlan asked.

"Aye. That!" Maggie nodded, pointing at Lochlan.

Keir laughed. "What are you talking about? The royals are nothing *but* hubris." Our guests both turned to Keir. "There're no guardrails on their behavior. Never have been." He flicked a glance at me. "Unless somebody hauls them into court, they do what they want. Even then, before Rita became magistrate, they'd just a pay a meaningless fine and go on about doing as they please."

That was a conversation stopper, and it wasn't easy to render Lochlan, Maggie, or myself speechless.

"Is there anything about this that will affect the upcoming court meet?" I asked.

Though Lochlan already knew the answer to the question, he ventured forth with a pointed look. "Are there any cases involving House of Bayune?"

"You know the answer is not only yes but fires of Hades yes. The kind of big, honking case that would be the sensational blowout feature of any magistrate's journal."

Lochlan sighed. "Though I only understood half of what was just said, I believe I've absorbed the gist."

"Good. Now what do we do?"

"I suggest we begin by requesting confirmation," Lochlan said.

"Via back channel." I said, matter-of-factly, that sentence being more observation than question.

Lochlan sighed.

Keir stepped in. "She means an inconspicuous inquiry."

"Oh." Lochlan nodded. To Maggie, he said, "We'd prefer to keep this between us at present. Can that be managed?"

"What are ye sayin', ye old fool? Are ye insinuatin' that I can no' keep a thing to myself?"

"Nothing of the kind, my dear. It's merely a formal agreement between the four of us to use utmost discretion and speak to no one else about our concerns. At present."

She harrumphed. "Very well. Why did ye no' just say so? I must be off. 'Twill be a busy night."

I was sorry to hear that. Death is seldom welcome, but much less so during the season of Yule.

I got up to see her out. "I'm glad you came by, Maggie. Stay warm."

"Oh, aye. No bother at all. I'm protected from the elements when on my rounds ye know."

I hadn't known that, but it made sense.

When she was gone, Keir poured coffee with Baileys for three. As I warmed my fingers on the mug, a question jumped to mind.

"Is Dairmuid married?"

Lochlan barked out a laugh then shared a look with Keir. "No," he shook his head and buried his face in his coffee mug.

My eyes locked on Keir's. "What is this about?"

Keir sighed. "If Diarmuid was human and part of the mundie world, he'd be known as a player."

"One who is highly sought after," Lochlan added.

Keir agreed with a nod. "If faerie published a gossip rag, his face would be on the cover every month with the title, 'Most Eligible Bachelor'."

"I see. Is that because he's really that desirable or because a lot of ambitious femmes see an opportunity to advance their status?"

"Bit o' both, I imagine," Lochlan answered.

"If Maeve hands over the crown, what will her role

be?"

"Hard to say," Keir started.

"Queen Mother," Lochlan said. Then added, "Creatrix in Chief? A faerie mound isn't a legitimate state without a creator in residence."

"How unusual are these creators?"

Keir mulled that over. "A lot of people can create, but only a few can create worlds. Like those reality show singing contests. Like that fellow on the telly said. A lot of people can sing, but only a few can rearrange the molecules in your body so that you have a visceral response."

I stared at Keir. It shouldn't continually surprise me how much was going on under that gorgeous tan and mass of blonde hair, and yet it did.

"When Diarmuid decides to marry, will he create a short list among the best, um, singers?"

"Hard to say," Lochlan jumped in. "We're in uncharted territory. Like we said, we haven't had a Di Anu for a very long time." I knew enough to know that when fae talked in terms of *very long time*, they meant when dinosaurs roamed the earth. "Who knows? He might even marry for love!"

He and Keir both shared a chuckle over that, like the idea was beyond preposterous.

"If Maeve remains an active part of the royal house," Lochlan continued, "and is willing to perform creative functions according to Diarmuid's will, there'll be no need to fill the position. He can continue… em…"

"Playing," I offered wryly.

"Yes. Well, I'll be off." Lochlan stood. "I'll grab my coat and thank you for the hearty supper."

"You're always welcome."

He pulled on his coat as he walked toward the front door with me. "The sephalian is a surprisingly good cook."

I agreed with a smile. "You know, he's good at everything he does." I glanced back to see if Keir overheard. It was fun to watch him preen at my praise and I made a mental note to tell him more often how much he was admired. By me. "Let's choose to not be overly anxious about this news. If Diarmuid is as reasonable as Maggie seems to think, we'll work it out. But it sounds like everything hinges on him *volunteering* to agree to abide by court decisions. We don't really have any teeth, do we?"

"Inside the courtroom? Yes. Outside the courtroom?

Sadly, no. Let's hope he believes it's in the best interest of all magic kind to maintain our somewhat tenuous hold on order. Because it is."

"By the way, do we have a designated diplomat?"

"In a manner of speaking. Me."

"Well, how could we do better than that?"

By the pleased look on Lochlan's face, I could tell I'd said the right thing.

When I closed the door behind him, I leaned my back against it and said, "Our just-the-two-of-us simple supper evening got hijacked."

Keir laughed softly. "But it's not a loss. Let's leave cleanup for Olivia and snuggle in for some quality shared sack time. Right after I raid the refrigerator. I'm starving."

"Sack time? Starving?" I giggled. "You're becoming more American by the day."

"No name calling."

"It was generous of you to share your sandwiches."

"I thought so." He nodded.

Olivia had made a fabulous turkey, chow mein noodles, mandarin orange casserole a couple of days before and only used half the turkey.

"I think there's half a turkey in there. Olivia sliced it and left it in the container with the red top."

"Half a turkey! Perfect!"

HAVING GOTTEN USED to our routine, the dogs padded into the bedroom ahead of us and flopped down by the fire. They were very polite and well-mannered when it came to ignoring lovemaking. And it was a good thing because otherwise I feel sure the sephalian would unceremoniously usher them to the other side of a closed door.

After two orgasms that made me see stars and an afterglow that included a full body lingering tingle, I whispered, "You're not worried, are you?"

"Not in the least. Nor should you be."

For the time being there was no better comfort to be had than Keir's quiet reassurance and I accepted it. Gladly. After all, he was an invaluable resource given his history with magic kind, particularly Irish fae. He had a working knowledge of their cultural perspective that was beyond me and perhaps always would be.

AFTER WALKING THE dogs and giving them a nice, hot

bowl of stuff I made especially for them, I set off to the shop in my red Wellies. When worn with cashmere socks from London, they were the perfect footwear for tromping about in snow, if you didn't have to go too far. I'd given up the magic shawl for winter and made my black, boiled wool coat my uniform. It looked great with my red rubber boots and I had a collection of winter scarves to create different looks.

Thoughts of enjoying winter, winter clothes, and extended morning snuggles with my ever warm sephalian kept my mind occupied all the way to the Hallows. I'd intended to stop by to see the new pieces and lend my opinion for whatever that's worth. Maggie and Dolan did wonders for my ego by always making me feel like my point of view added something worthwhile.

I hadn't planned to stay long because stacks of briefs were calling, but one of the new arrivals was a wonder. There, in the center of the center work table, sat a three-foot-long recreation of the Egyptian sphinx. Only this one was covered in stylized scales that looked like real gold, had huge sapphires for eyes, and wasn't missing its nose.

"Is that real gold?"

"Aye," Maggie said. "The good stuff. No' that droch mix o' cheap metals modern humans try to pass off as gold."

"Hmmm. I'm no connoisseur, but there's no question that it looks different. It's so…"

"Pretty. Is it no'?'

"Oh, yes. It certainly is. For one thing the color is more coppery, less yellow." I was thinking that I could almost understand why wars had been fought over the stuff. It was beautiful enough to mesmerize. "And it's a magical artifact?"

"Aye."

"How old?"

"Old."

"So, was the sphinx at Giza a copy of this or the other way around?"

Maggie looked amused. "'Tis the big one in the desert that's the copy."

"So, what does it do?"

"Do?" Maggie sounded confused.

In a rare vocal moment, Dolan treated us to a rush of words. "She means does it get up and dance or grant wishes or guard against hauntings or such."

Maggie and I both stared at Dolan for a few beats.

Finally, Maggie looked at me and said, "Is that what you meant?"

It was a fairly good description of what I meant, but it sounded so stupid I was reluctant to own up to it.

"Well…"

"The thing about magical artifacts," Dolan interrupted, "is that it's nigh to impossible to know what they'll do, if anything, until they do it. They don't come with an instruction manual."

That was flawlessly sensical.

"Of course. I will withdraw that question and pose another. That being the case, how do we know that a new piece doesn't have something unwanted attached?"

"Like doom?" Maggie asked cheerfully.

"Um. Well. I was hoping for something less catastrophic. Is doom a possibility?"

Dolan looked at Maggie. "She's been here for months and is just now wondering that."

"That's true, Dolan," I said. "What is also true is that you didn't answer my question. And that you're talking about me like I'm not here."

"Well," Maggie began, "though 'tis true that we'll usually no' be knowin' the nature of a thing till it decides to reveal itself, 'tis also true that we've been keepin' the shop and acceptin' deliveries for a good, long while. The fact that we're still here is a ripe good indication that the sender of antiquities has no malice in mind. Ye might say we've established a…"

"Track record?"

"Aye. Track record. But o' course ye ne'er know. Every new day is a…"

"Leap of trust," Dolan said.

My gaze jerked to his. "Trust in the *totally* anonymous, *totally* mysterious person or persons who sends us things to sell without expecting anything in return?"

"Just so," Maggie said with a satisfaction indicating she believed the matter was neatly sewn up and tied with a bow.

"Right. Why would we question that?"

I had to place Maggie's cavalier perspective within the context of a person who was perhaps immortal and, at the very least, hard to kill.

Then she went on, "But 'tis no' entirely accurate to say a thing ne'er arrives with an instruction manual. A few times there have been notes attached. Brief and cryptic, they are, but suggestin' caution when needed."

"I just realized that our customers enter into this Russian Roulette game with us, don't they? When a piece such as this is acquired, they take it home not knowing its nature, what it's capable of, or what might be the trigger to set off who-knows-what."

"Exactly right! Part of the fun of it, I suppose," Maggie said brightly. "It's our day for lunch at your house. What are we havin'?"

Dolan had lost interest in the conversation and gone back to work.

"I didn't ask," I said absently while doing a mental inventory of items I'd taken home. "Do I have any of the magical pieces in my house? The ones that we trust are not ticking time bombs, but might still go boom?"

"Just the love god statue."

"Eros."

"That's the one."

"And we have no idea what it might, um, do."

"We have no reason to think 'twill do anythin'. Unless that might be to bring you happiness." She leaned in conspiratorially. "In a romancin' kind of way I mean."

Ignoring that, I said, "What about the hobknobbit? It didn't come with a warning."

"No. It did no'," Maggie looked more serious. "But our conclusion, our sense of the thing, was that it did no' originate with our primary source."

"Someone slipped it in and made it seem like it was a normal shipment from your regular mysterious and anonymous source."

"Aye. The hobknobbit was a goat tryin' to pass itself off as a sheep."

"Are you saying goats are bad? Sheep are good?"

I heard Dolan laugh out loud all the way from the workroom and wondered if his ears were good enough to have heard what was just said.

"Noooo." Maggie drew out the word like she was exercising patience with a child. "I'm sayin' the item was different. We do no' have enough reason to pronounce the thing evil. Just a niggle of a suspicion. The fact that 'twas buried under a mountain of salt in the vampire's basement was just a precautionary measure."

"Right." I inhaled deeply, deciding that I'd spent enough time in the shop. "I'll leave you to it and go back to reviewing cases for the Solstice Court."

"Oh, sure. How's that goin'?"

"It seems far less bizarre than the first time. Maybe the fantastic is becoming my normal."

"There you have it then." Her eyes lit up. "Any interestin' cases you'd be wantin' to share?"

I laughed. "Maggie. It wouldn't be in keeping with my office to discuss the cases ahead of court. And you know it."

"Aye. But you can no' blame a lass for tryin'."

I stopped by Esme's just to say hello. As usual she acted like she wasn't excited to see me, but I knew it was pretense. She loved my visits, no matter how brief.

"Esme. Do you know something about how the Hallows gets its inventory?"

"I know some… thing," she said cautiously.

"What I want to know is, do we have any reason to be worried about artifact deliveries?"

She looked curious, which was noteworthy, because

any display of emotion was unusual for Esmerelda.

"Why do you ask?"

"Because it occurred to me this morning that our wares don't arrive with a certificate of authenticity or a history of any kind. We really don't know anything about them. Not what they are, where they came from, line of ownership, or how they might affect the owner or their surroundings."

"But you do have Dolan. Do you have reason to doubt his sensory awareness?"

"No. I didn't know we were relying on Dolan's, um, sensory awareness. You mean because he identified the hobknobbit thing as questionable?"

"As a recent example. Yes. His assessments have proven reliable. And why would you worry?"

"Well, for one thing, I don't want the shop or my associates brought to ruin."

Esmerelda treated me to a rare laugh. "Rita. Your gift for overstatement is exquisite."

"Think so? That was toned down. Maggie used the word 'doom'."

Esme waved that off as she shook her head. "Well,

Maggie is Maggie."

"I don't know how to argue with that. But doom trumps ruin. Unfortunate might be the destruction of the Hallows' workroom. Tragedy might be the end of the shop. Ruin might destroy Hallow Hill. Doom could mean the destruction of all Britain."

She cocked her head. "You've thought this through, have you?"

"Um. Not really?"

"Surprising. I was expecting that next you'd be pulling a color-coded catastrophe chart with graphs out of your bag."

Esme was mistress of whipping up spontaneous word salads with snark so thick it could hang in the air for hours.

"What would you know about charts and graphs?" I knew better than to banter with Esmerelda, but I was often hairbrained enough to blurt out a retort without due consideration.

She was nonplussed. Of course. "From what I understand of recent developments, you have enough to fret over without adding artifact anxiety to the mix."

That could only mean the gossip mill was churning. "You heard about the…"

"Succession. Yes."

"Possible succession."

"Ogre dung. It's a fait accompli."

"You're sure?"

"Positive."

"Well, that's confirmation enough for me." I thought I saw a ghost of a smile. "Okay. Later."

"Yes. I'll be there for lunch."

"Oh. You're coming today? Good. See you then."

CHAPTER THREE

Joy to the Juiced

I WAS UNWINDING my Burberry-like scarf as I entered my kitchen.

"Wow, Olivia. You may have outdone yourself today." I was referring to the heavenly smells that filled the house.

She smiled. "You say that every day."

I chuckled. "It's not schmooze. I say that because it's what I'm thinking. What is it?"

"Lamb loin smothered in onions and peppercorn sauce. Braised asparagus tips. Whipped potatoes. Personal baguettes."

"Baguettes? That French bread that explodes, sending crumbs everywhere when you touch it?"

She smiled indulgently. "Yes. I suppose it does that. But it's good. Your guests like it. And I will tidy up. Of course."

I looked down at my black knit sweater and decided to change into something light-colored with a tight silky weave that crumbs wouldn't cling to.

"Thanks for the heads up."

"Okay," she said.

That was when I noticed the table was set for seven. It was designed to seat six, but we could squeeze without much trouble.

"We have an extra today?"

"Fie asked to come just a bit ago. Is that okay?"

"Of course, Liv. You're the one who bears the burden."

I DON'T KNOW why Lochlan thought he had a prayer of keeping the transfer of the Irish crown under wraps. It was apparent that *everybody* knew. That being the case, no one could talk about anything else at lunch.

Fie turned to me just as I had half an individual-sized baguette sticking out of my mouth and asked, "What will you do if there's a case involving the Irish and Diarmuid doesn't comply?"

Rather than proceeding with biting off a hunk of

bread, chewing, and swallowing while everyone was waiting and watching, I chose to back the baguette out of my mouth with as much ladylike grace as possible.

"I'm hoping it never comes to that, Fie. But I have confidence in my advisors and feel certain they'll always help guide me to the best outcomes."

"Brava," Fie said. "That was as masterful a political statement as I've ever heard." He turned to the others. "Call the press. She's ready."

"Are you making fun of me?" I asked him.

"Certainly not. I'd sooner cut off a finger than risk offending the host of Hallow Hill's famed lunch salon."

I laughed. "Lunch salon?"

At this point I rose impulsively to fetch wine from the cooler. Seven people. I grabbed two bottles and handed them to Keir wordlessly while Olivia, without being told, glided toward the crystal cabinet to retrieve seven wine glasses. We were like a team of telepaths. One mind. One goal – keep me out of trouble by turning on the happy spigot.

"Sure," Fie continued. "Your lunches are famous for the best food in the world." He glanced at Olivia to be sure she'd heard the compliment. "But your guests also talk about news and ideas." As Olivia rose to clear plates and ready the table for dessert, Fie said, "This transfer of power is news. Definitely. And I'm curious about your thoughts."

"Honestly, Fie, at this point anything we discuss is hypothetical. When we have more information about what this might mean," I looked around the table, "to all of us, I'll join in the discussion."

"Promise?" he asked.

"Promise. What's got you worried?"

"Upheaval."

I nodded. "Nobody likes that. But let's look on the bright side. I don't imagine the Irish fae want war any more than anyone else."

Everyone stopped stock still. After a very uncomfortable pause, Fie said, "War?"

Uh oh.

"Pay no attention to me." I tried to cover. "I'm taking outlandish lessons from Maggie."

When everyone laughed, I felt a huge sigh of relief that the red herring I'd plunked onto the table had worked. Keir was the only person at lunch who knew there was an actual threat of actual war on the actual horizon. But he could be completely unreadable when he chose to be.

This was yet another good reason, among many, why it was lucky that I'd fallen for an officer of the court. If he was somebody else, I wouldn't be able to freely share all the behind-the-scenes machinations necessary to make the wheel of justice turn in the right direction.

I took the bottle Keir had just opened and began to pour wine.

"We never have wine at lunch," Fie observed.

I shrugged and smiled. "What's the holiday season for if not wine at lunch?" I was eager to keep the conversation steered in a harmless direction, "Did anybody else notice that it snowed last night?"

I wasn't above distracting people with divine juice and talk of weather.

THERE'D BEEN A flaw in my plan to be sure. The problem with the wine part of wining and dining is that I'm as susceptible to the effects of the sacred grape as the next person, and probably much more so than magic kind.

The after-lunch drowsiness that was normal for me

was amplified by the wine and the word "nap" was flashing across the screen of my mind.

I told myself that I'd read at least one more brief before giving into the desire to curl up under the faux fur blanket and check out.

SITTING DOWN AT my study table I lifted the next file on top of the stack and opened it at the same time my bum connected with the chair. There was a handwritten Post-it note from Lochlan on the inside cover. It seemed there was a second case that had the potential to make groundbreaking precedent.

The Valkyrie, Sigrid, had petitioned the Council of Asgard with her desire to retire. They'd said no. But rather than drop the matter, she did what no one else had ever done. She filed a lawsuit. The Norse gods were not subject to the fae justice system, but as the result of a brilliant argument made by the Bureau of Behavioral Oversight, they'd agreed to participate and abide by my ruling.

Oh, my gods.

In deference to the old ones from whom all power originated and their shared origins with fae, they'd allow

Sigrid to make her case and would send someone to represent the Council.

Oh, my gods!

I'd been falling asleep when I began reading the brief but was wide awake by the time I finished. There was to be an actual god in my courtroom submitting to my judgment? It was too much. Was I hyperventilating or just experiencing palpitations? Or was that both at the same time?

I looked down to see both dogs at my side staring at me with what I imagined was a canine expression of concern. By twisting my body into a pretzel shape, I was able to reach out and pet them both at the same time.

"No worries my little loves," I murmured. "I've just been tossed into the deep end and it's one of those only-way-out-is-through things."

Keir appeared at the door. "Talking to the kids?"

He called them that sometimes.

"Maybe I need to get one of those cuff contraptions to take my own blood pressure."

"Rita. There's nothing wrong with you. What's the problem?"

I told him about the case of the Valkyrie and the fact that an actual Norse god might be making an appearance before me, as Asgard's defence.

Keir shrugged. "He puts his pants on one leg at a time."

I gave him a look. "Do you know that to be true?"

"Not in the least. I was trying to say something helpful." I groaned. "We're in for an interesting Solstice Court, aren't we?"

"Interesting could be one of your bigger understatements. We're going to have somebody at court meet who can't be enforced." My eyes flew to Keir. "Can he?"

"If you mean would I be eager to confront a Norse god, the answer is definitely not. For one thing, they're capable of appearing and disappearing at will. How do you fight somebody like that? Supposedly, my power on the grounds of Tregeagle is absolute, but I wouldn't want to test it."

"Wonder who they'll send?"

"Just as long as it's not Loki. If there's truth in the tales of his character and exploits, he'll probably ask for the job. His history leaves the impression that he's an attention-hog. He'd probably cause so many problems for us that we'd never dare meddle in their affairs again. That approach would be close to genius, wouldn't it? They could say they cooperated fully while at the same time insuring it's a one off."

"Great. Just what I need in my court. A god who likes to act out."

"Confer with Lochlan. See if you can open some diplomatic channels and set some ground rules for conduct ahead of time."

"Keir!" I jumped up to rush him and pepper his face with kisses of reward. "That is positively brilliant. I'm going to go right over and discuss it with Lochlan." I nodded. "Just as soon as I get up from my nap."

I'D SET THE alarm on my phone to alert me at 5:15. I'd made a chart of times I'd be most likely to catch Evie taking into account her class days and times and the time difference. When I heard the pleasant little chime, I stopped and called.

"Mom!"

I loved that she sounded glad to hear from me.

"Yes, precious."

"I can't believe you got me a first-class ticket! This is going to be *so* amazing. Can we afford that?"

I chuckled at her choice of pronoun. "Yeah. *We* can. You're going to love traveling in style."

"I was born to be rich. I've always known that it was an accident that I was delivered to a middleclass family, but fate finally recognized the mistake and got busy correcting it." Oddly enough, she wasn't *completely* wrong. "Seriously. Any packing suggestions?"

"It snows here every day so that it's perpetually pristine and looks like a storybook." She hummed dreamily in response. "So warm stuff. Waterproof boots. What do you want from Santa?"

"Wow. What I'd like most is to believe in Santa again."

"Don't get me started. It's one of those parental conflicts that I'm still agonizing over. Still not sure if it was the best choice to lie to my kid about a jolly elf, miniature sleigh, and eight tiny reindeer. It breeds mistrust and cynicism."

She laughed. "You agonize over that? Wow, Mom, you should take parenting less seriously. Millions of people have survived learning that Santa is a lovely figment of imagination. Annnnnnd, I'm not a cynic."

"Well, in any case, I can't give you belief in Santa. What else do you want?"

"A new boyfriend."

"You're making me long for the days when the answer was Easy Bake oven or ten-speed bike. What happened to Harrison?"

"You are way behind. Harrison was two jerks ago."

"Well, I can't know that if you don't tell me."

"I didn't tell you? Well, I'm in between men and my love life sucks."

Men?

"You worry about schoolwork. *Men* can wait."

"Schoolwork is the one thing I don't have to worry about. I'm, um, good at it."

"I know you are."

"As a matter of fact, I have news."

"What?"

"I've scored a spot at Oxford! Starting next summer. If the money really isn't an obstacle? Like you said?"

"Oxford?" Pause. "Oxford, England?"

"No. Oxford, Mississippi." She chuckled. "Of course, Oxford, England. I looked it up. I'd be just like an hour's drive away."

"Ah…"

"Wouldn't it be great to be so close?"

"Ah. An hour. Away. Is really close." Was this what deer felt like when headlights are coming straight at them? "That would be…"

"Unbelievable!"

"Just the word I was looking for."

"Yeah. And just think how good that's gonna look on my rap sheet."

"Your rap sheet?"

"You know. My resume. Someday I'm gonna wanna teach."

I tried to get an image of Evie teaching and failed, but wouldn't want to undermine my kid's aspirations. So, I decided on a complete noncommittal, "Right."

"So maybe when I'm visiting, we can go look around? Oxford, I mean?"

"Well, I…"

"So that's what I want from Santa. A free ride to Oxford and no student loans! Oh, Mom, Jules is doing some kind of frantic motioning thing. I guess I should go. I could call you back?"

"That's okay. Take care. We'll talk in a couple of days."

When I'd moved to Hallow Hill, I'd told Lochlan there was zero chance that my daughter would move to England. I should have known better than to talk in absolutes. That's not the part that concerned me most. Obviously. The part that concerned me most would be managing my magical life with a mundie daughter popping in from time to time.

Reminding myself to breathe, I looked at the dogs. "Another fine mess I've gotten myself into." Frey's left ear twitched like hearing that was offensive. "I don't mean *you*. You're a *joy*. I mean," I waved at the air, "everything else."

That was when I chose to confront how much I hadn't shared. Maybe I didn't know about two boyfriends since Harrison. But Evie didn't know about Keir, my dogs, or my job magistrating magical disputes.

"Talking to the hounds again?" Keir appeared at my door and sounded amused.

"I have extremely valid reasons to go off the deep end. If you find me wandering in the snow in my moose slippers mumbling about Santa, it's because my daughter is going to drive me to drink."

"What happened?"

After retelling the conversation, word for word, to the best of my recollection, he said, "Coffee with Baileys?"

I was so tempted.

"I'd like to spend the rest of December joyfully juiced, but I'm a big girl and have to face the fact that Bailey's is a temporary solution at best."

He pulled me up to a standing position. "Hug then?"

I grinned as I slipped into an embrace that always felt like we were two puzzle pieces locking securely into place. "You give the *best* hugs."

He chuckled as he lowered his head and nuzzled my neck. "I was thinking the same thing about you." Nip. Kiss. Nuzzle some more. "You know everybody in Hallow Hill loves you. If we all must pretend when she visits, even if it's often, we will. All the world's a stage you know."

I sighed and pulled back. "That's a lovely thought and very much appreciated, but it does nothing to account for what goes on at court meets. Or the time I spend preparing for them."

"We'll figure it out." He smiled. "I'm looking forward to meeting her."

"Um."

"Um?"

"She doesn't know about you." His smile fell away. "Yet! I mean, *yet*."

"You haven't told her you're in a relationship? A *serious*, live-together relationship? Or you haven't told her about me at all?"

"Haven't told her about you at all," I said sheepishly.

His face went void of emotion, which meant he'd shut down all display of emotion and was not allowing me to get a read.

Uh oh.

"Please don't have your feelings hurt. I'm going to correct it. She doesn't know about my dogs either!"

His stone face faltered and he gaped. "You're comparing me to the dogs?"

"Of course not. I'm just saying that, when I talk to her, she's always in the middle of something or on the way from here to there. And rushed. There just hasn't been an ideal time to introduce sensitive subjects."

"Rita."

"I know! I'll make sure she's up to speed before she gets here. Promise. I wouldn't subject us to the chaos of that many surprises all at once. I'm much more mature than that."

It didn't escape me that he looked dubious. I wasn't sure if that was about my promise to come clean or my declaration of maturity, but I wasn't thrilled about having either of those things viewed as doubtful. Recognizing that it wasn't a good time to chase rabbits, I let it go while silently giving myself kudos for maturity.

THREE DAYS LATER I had another opportunity to relish a bit of "alone time" in the house, dogs excepted, of course. I'd made myself a ginger tea and indulged in the peace of watching big fluffy snowflakes drift to earth and settle with their brethren to make visual magic. The quiet in the house was delicious.

Awareness of the one unread brief left on the table nagged at me until I diverted my attention from staring out the window and picked up the brown folder. I'd just opened it when my front door alerted me not to turn around. Oh. Oh.

The dogs were at the front door first and the fact that they were wagging their tails made me assume the visitor was someone they knew and approved of.

I swung open the door expecting to see Lochlan and was instead blindsided by the appearance of the alleged new king of Irish fae. None other than Diarmuid, himself, stood on my porch wearing a red and purple tartan scarf and snow in his hair. After acknowledging me with a curt nod and a smile, his eyes dropped to the dogs who'd stepped over the threshold in welcome and were wiggling joyfully.

"Greetin's, pups," he said cheerfully as he bent to give each of them a rousing petting, which appeared to make them ecstatic. "A very fine brace of fraighounds you have here. How old?"

"Eight weeks," I answered dumbly. "They, um, grow fast," I said, like he wouldn't know that.

Rising to his full height, which meant that he was towering over me, he said, "Well, Magistrate. Will you have me in or no'?"

I hesitated. For one thing it didn't seem fitting to entertain someone of Diarmuid's royal stature while in my moose slippers. On the other hand, he hadn't called ahead.

I couldn't deny that his smile was both charming and disarming.

I couldn't deny that my dogs liked him. A lot.

I knew it might not be the most prudent decision of my life, but I also thought turning Diarmuid away from my door might be political suicide. The snow was falling harder so that it almost looked like a curtain beyond the covered porch and I was sure the open door was cooling the entire house. All this was probably playing out on my face while he waited patiently.

"Of course. Come in." I stepped back, opened the door to its full width and invited him in. "Let me light the fires." Since I'd been in the study, the living room fire hadn't been lit all day and the kitchen fire had gone cold after Olivia finished up. "And start the kettle. A hot cup will warm you right up."

He seemed amused by the suggestion that he needed warming up. I supposed he could control his temperature, but my hospitality chops were pure human and set in their ways.

"'Twould be nice. Thank you." He looked around. "A nice house, Magistrate. Very... Very."

I wasn't sure how to respond to 'very, very', but said, "Thank you. You know the builder well."

"Do I?" He asked with a slight cock of his head.

"Your mother."

"Ah." He laughed then took a closer look as he followed me toward the kitchen. "Then this is the house of your heart."

"So, I'm told. Lochlan said that very thing when it was created."

"Good ole Lochlan."

"I suppose you've known him a long time."

"Dependin' on your point of view. I've known him all my life."

"In truth then, for you, that's the entirety of time."

"Why, Magistrate, you're a deep thinker."

I laughed. "I'm not accused of that every day. I assure you. What sort of warmup do you prefer? Coffee? Chocolate? I have several kinds of tea and could manage a hot chicken broth if you're peckish."

He shook his head amiably as he removed the scarf and draped it over one of my island barstools. "What will you be havin'?"

I stopped and focused on my visitor. "Tell me the occasion for your visit and I'll tell you what I'm having."

He laughed again. "May I sit?" He motioned toward one of the chairs at my round table that was near the fire. I gave permission with a nod and an open palm gesture toward the chair. He sat and said, "Is this a replica of the Arthurian round table?"

He sounded incredulous.

"Yes. The man, or, rather brounie, who works at The Hallows made it for me."

"I want one just like it. Maybe a wee bit bigger."

"I'm sure your mum can arrange that."

"Aye. No doubt." He sounded wistful. "Came to my attention that there's concern about me havin' nabbed the Fengall sprite. I thought I'd forego the diplomacy thing and jump right to frankness between you and me. I'd been intendin' to come by anyway. To make sure no hard feelin's had followed that business with the kelpies."

"Well, since you mention it, I am a little surprised at your overture since our first and only encounter ended with a ruling against you."

He laughed. "Is that how you see it?"

I blinked. "Um, yes. Isn't that how everybody sees it?"

He shook his head. "No. No' at all. Niall does no' have the sense to know when to wipe his arse or for how long. He should've been whipped for that stunt. Next time he will be whether you order it or no'. When Bayune is brought into court 'tis my responsibility to mount a defense, even if it's perfunctory, and even if the family member is a ne'er-do-well miscreant such as my little brother. I found your handlin' of the matter admirable."

I blinked again. "Um. That's surprising, but welcome news. I don't want to be at odds with the House of Bayune *needlessly*." I added the last word to make the point that I'm not opposed to being at odds with the House of Bayune if the situation called for it. No number of friendly fireside chats would change that.

"Understood."

Most of the tension left my body when I realized he'd come to do bridge-building. Personally. It was a promising beginning.

"In that case, I'm having ridiculously naughty coffee. That means real, honest-to gods cream. Not half and half. Not 'creamer'," I used air quotes with the most powerful fae in the world. Shamelessly. "I'll make it Yule-festive with a tiny splash of peppermint. If we're going to come to a meeting of the minds, we need a celebration drink."

Diarmuid's grin either caused a tiny hallucination or a trick of the light. Because for a moment I was sure all my festive, white, Yule decoration bulbs, that were set to steady glow, did a curious twinkle thing to match the flare of light in his blue eyes.

"You think coffee is naughty, Magistrate?" The implication that I had no comprehension of the meaning of 'naughty' hung heavily in the air. "No matter. 'Tis a fine suggestion. The house drink of choice is what I'll be havin' as well."

"Excellent." As I set about making coffee, I said, "How did you know I'd be here by myself? Or was it an accident?"

"Oh, no. 'Twas no accident. I had crows watchin' the house for the right opportunity."

I stopped and turned. "Crows?"

The idea of being spied on by birds was unsettling. I had windows.

"Aye. Marvelous creatures really. Colorful ye might say."

"Really."

I set cream, peppermint, enormous penguin mugs, spoons, napkins, and Olivia's holiday cookies on the table, left the percolator gurgling happily, and sat down. When I pushed the cookies, or biscuits as they're called in the Kingdom, closer to Diarmuid, he took one. I'd learned over the past couple months that Olivia's food was magic because it had the effect of making people feel sated, secure, and happy. I made a mental note to make Olivia's food an integral part of any important conversation.

"Hmm. These are good!" He didn't take his eyes away from the plate of cookies. "You made these?"

"No. I have a caretaker who also cooks." When he looked up with a gleam in his eye, I said, "Do not even think about it. Poaching other people's domestic help is a good way to start a war."

I'd intended that as figurative banter but was instantly

sorry to have made such an impolitic remark.

I was wondering just how stupid I could be, when he said, "War." I blinked. "'Tis one of the things I came to discuss."

The percolator chose that moment to reach its climax, which rivaled a cross between espresso hissing and Desdemona's death scene in *Othello*.

"Hold that thought." I punctuated that with a raised index finger. "And please don't be bashful about the cookies. There're more where those came from."

In less than a minute I was back with the pot pouring coffee that smelled heavenly if I did say so myself.

"You were saying?"

"I understand there was some concern about resolution of this thing with the House of Ulfrwulf."

"You make saying that sound so easy. I don't think I'll ever get the pronunciation right. But yes. There's been some concern."

"Well. 'Tis all patted out and in the past." He smiled brightly.

"Patted out?"

"Aye. Ye might say a settlement's been reached.

Agreeable to all parties."

"So your bunch is happy. Queen Ilmr, too?"

"My 'bunch' is happy. Aye. No' sure it can be said that Ilmr's e'er been happy so that's a stretch too far. 'Tis no' an outright criticism though. I suppose one would have to be on the stern side to keep Northmen in line. They're almost as unruly as Irish."

"You won't be going with the stern style?"

"Well," he drawled, in a pretending-to-be-humble kind of way, "'tis different for me. Leadership is more easily accepted from males than females." He shrugged. "'Tis the way of it."

I really, really, really wished I could argue with that. "So, the takeaway is that the dispute's been resolved, large scale conflict averted. That's very good news and a huge relief."

"Aye. 'Tis."

"Might I ask how you brought about this understand-ing?"

"I can no' take all the credit personally. You must un-derstand that the sprite was taken and brought back to Ireland just to make a point. We ne'er intended to keep

VICTORIA DANANN

her. 'Twas a matter of savin' face for my mother, ye know. 'Twas always to be temporary. A harmless statement. Nothin' more."

"I see. So, you returned the sprite and all is well."

"I did no'. My cousin is returnin' *with* the sprite. Seems they're in love!"

He rolled his eyes in a universally understood gesture of have-you-ever-heard-of-*anything*-more-lame?

"In, um, love?"

"Aye. Irish faerie is too mild for Eevi. That's the name of the snow sprite. And Cass says he can no' live without her. Poor devil. So, he's goin' there to live." Diarmuid nabbed another cookie and ate half. "'Tis like those human royal alliances. We can no' go to war with them now because one of us is part of their court."

"I see," I repeated. "Well, lucky for us. Long live love."

Diarmuid barked out a laugh. "So, they say."

"I'm getting that you're not a fan. Of love."

"No' this sort. Romantic love. 'Tis pure pish and middle. An excuse for people grown too lazy to look for their next…" He hesitated as if searching for a polite word and finally settled on, "Encounter. O' course, for a person such

108

as myself with an unlimited supply of eager partners, there's no' much effort expended."

His self-satisfied chuckle left no doubt that fae don't consider vanity a fault.

"Congratulations, Diarmuid. I believe you just won my prize for most cynical statement I've ever heard. As in *ever*." Thinking this line of dialogue was going nowhere, I changed the subject. "So, it's true that you're about to be crowned king?"

"No 'about' to it. 'Tis done."

I inhaled deeply. "My courtly manners education is in the early stages. Am I supposed to address you with some sort of honorific now? Your Highness or Your Majesty or Di Anu?"

With a surprised chuckle, he said, "This is the first mention of Di Anu that I've heard. 'Tis what people are sayin?"

"Some. I suppose."

"Hmmm. Well. Diarmuid's fine. Technically you and I are equals."

I doubted that anyone in faerie would see Diarmuid and I as equals, but it wasn't a point I wanted to argue.

"Does this mean that, going forward, you'll agree to submit to the judgments of the court?"

He looked stupefied. "O' course. What else would ye be thinkin'? I'm no' foolhardy nor shortsighted. The future of our race depends on keepin' faith with our recent institutional progress. Even if the structure's a wee bit more flexible than you're used to, 'tis what humans call a guardrail.

"'Twould no' be in the best interest of fae to mount idiotic little skirmishes. The world, includin' faerie, has changed. We'll adapt. No' just survive. But thrive."

My respect for Diarmuid was growing by the minute. I didn't know if I could legitimately be called a deep thinker, but the new king appeared to be the real deal.

The mudroom door opened and closed. I heard Keir stomp twice and tracked the sound of his approaching steps.

Naturally, he was surprised to see Diarmuid sitting in the kitchen having coffee.

"Look who's here," I said nonchalantly.

"Afternoon, little brother," Diarmuid said.

Keir's eyes slid from the king to me. "All good?"

"Better than good. We've averted a war and set up diplomatic channels."

"Have we now?" Keir looked at Diarmuid.

"Yes," I said. "And guess what else? Diarmuid is king."

"Um-hum," Keir responded.

Diarmuid got to his feet. "I was just goin'."

"I'm a little curious." I stopped him with another question. "You don't have to answer, of course, but I have to ask. Why is Maeve stepping aside?"

His eyes flicked to Keir before he smiled and said, "Sorry, Magistrate. Family business."

"Okay. Had to ask. It was a good idea you had," I said, also rising, "talking face to face."

"Saves time," he said.

"It does." I walked him to the front door. "Well, you know where to find me. But I don't like the bird spying thing."

His brow crinkled slightly, like he was confused. "What do you mean? 'Tis what birds do."

I blinked. "Are you saying all birds spy on people?"

"Well, aye. O' course. They do no' report what they see unless someone such as myself asks. Hard to work with at times. They're extraordinarily particular about the phrasin' of questions and they're deliberately cryptic and misleadin' with their answers."

"The phrasing of questions," I repeated drily. I felt my final tether to reality as I'd known it slipping out of reach. "Right. What do you offer them in return?"

He laughed. "We'll have a good reign together, Magistrate."

"Just let the crows know that, if I see them around here in the future, I may become very interested in shotguns."

"Were it no' for their valuable insights, I'd be pleased to join you in that pastime."

I glanced behind me to see Keir's reaction, but he wasn't there. When I turned back to the door, Diarmuid was gone and there were no prints in the fresh snow.

I shuffled back to the kitchen. Keir was in the kitchen putting a kettle on the stove.

"He called you brother," I said.

"I heard," he replied without looking up.

"Are you, um, upset about his visit?"

He stood up straighter then turned to look at me.

"Should I be?"

"Of course not."

"Alright then."

"Keir, what is this? You're not jealous of Diarmuid. Is this about me or is it a sibling rivalry thing?"

After a small, but exasperated huff, he said, "I didn't like coming home to find him sitting in *our* kitchen."

I couldn't help but feel a little thrill of feminine satisfaction. The sephalian who shared my bed was worried that the fae world's most eligible bachelor was interested in me. In that way. And he called the kitchen "our" kitchen. That made my tummy warm.

Annnnnnd. *Wow.* It had been less than three months since I was a lower income insurance adjuster with unpaid bills and no marital love life or companionship to speak of. Today I had the most interesting people in Hallow Hill for lunch, had the king of Irish fae for coffee in my kitchen, and then had the most desirable male in existence act jealous about it. And, as my daughter pointed out, I'm rich.

Life had definitely taken a turn for the better.

"He's just trying to pave the way for amiable relations

with the court. He told me to call him Diarmuid and said he thinks of me as an equal."

Keir smirked. "Yes. And the bloody blaggard called me brother, too."

"What's wrong with that?"

"The bother is that I don't remember him having ever spoken to me before. Or acknowledging me in any way. He's cunning. Sly. And wants something."

"I won't dismiss that as a possibility. I agree I shouldn't be too quick to trust. I'll keep my guard up. For one thing, I can't be thought of as fraternizing with various contingents. It would make people see partiality in rulings even when there was none."

Hearing that seemed to make Keir relax visibly.

"Exactly," he said. "And he has a cartoon face."

I barked out a laugh. This should be good. "What's a cartoon face?"

With an exasperated twist of his body, he said, "You know," and twirled a finger in the air. "Everything is too much." When I continued to look blank, he expounded, "Chin too square. Dimple too deep. Eyes too blue. Hair always in place. Like that."

"Oh. I see." And I really did. I remembered a day when I'd seen Aoumeil on the sidewalk with Keir and began trying to imagine life without him. "I can't stand it when you're out of sorts. What can I do to make you smile?"

The look he gave me was suggestive enough to set the house on fire.

I chuckled. "So, you're feeling *that* needy and insecure, are you?"

"I'm neither needy nor insecure. I'm just a male with a pressing need to re-stake my claim."

"And the best way to do that is to…"

"Make sure my smell is all over you."

"You know," I began as I walked toward him. "There's something kind of erotic and forbidden about making love to a man with animal instincts."

He chuckled softly. "Animal instincts, is it?"

After a series of feverish kisses coupled with sincere reassurances that, in my eyes, no one could possibly measure up to Keir Culain, we shared a soapy shower, some laughter, and got ready to go to the pub.

Dinner was later than usual, but my lover was relaxed,

cheerful, and full of the self-confidence I was used to seeing him wear like a second skin. It had stopped snowing at dark. Shortly thereafter the clouds drifted away so that the sky was a black background for stars that twinkled more spectacularly than any holiday lights.

We stopped by Lochlan's house before we set out for the pub so that I could deliver the news that Diarmuid was indeed king and that war was no longer a possibility. My clerk was perhaps even more pleased than I. The combination of personal experience with my neighbors and the informal education I'd received, courtesy of the big book, I gleaned that elves and pixies had a strong preference for good times. And peace is the underpinning of good times. One isn't possible without the other except for the occasional psychopath of the Batman villain sort, the kind who'd welcome end times.

CHAPTER FOUR

Joel Kinnaman

"THE SPELL'S BEEN lifted."

That was Lochlan's greeting as my dogs joined their parents on the hill above our shared lane. We must've been a sight to magic kind. An elf, a shivering, cold human, and a pack of wolves romping and playing together on the moors in the early morning frost like they thought it was heaven.

"Spell?" I asked absently before understanding his meaning. "Oh! You mean I can read about the Wild Hunt and remember what I read now?"

"Yes. If you have questions, Keir can help sort you out."

"Keir? Is he an authority?"

Lochlan chuckled. "Perhaps not in the sense that you

mean, but the sephalian is associated with Bayune. He'd be considered an insider in most circles."

"Well, the good luck just keeps coming my way." That was intended to be a genuinely cheerful observation, but it didn't come out sounding that way. My elf friend didn't seemed too distracted to notice. "What am I missing, Lochlan?"

"What? Oh. Nothing at all. At times I'm uncertain about interpreting your side of a conversation."

"Huh. Is it the snark or the sarcasm?" He opened his mouth, but nothing came out. "Maybe it's the cynicism." I snapped my fingers. "No! It's the stupidity!"

Lochlan looked dumbstruck. It seemed that self-deprecation was even more bewildering than snark, sarcasm, and cynicism.

I chuckled hoping to put him at ease. "Honestly, I struggle with the British sense of humor and slang. It's clear that's a two-way road. But since I'm in the land of left side driving, I'll make a bigger effort to be understood."

"I'm not a stuffed shirt." I hated that I'd made him feel defensive. "I understood that joke you made about nobody expecting the Spanish Inquisition."

I felt a barmaid's laugh bark out of my diaphragm, and was a little surprised to realize that bawdy sound came from me.

"Lochlan. You thought that was funny because it doesn't get more British than *Monty Python*. Believe me, not many Americans are made hysterical by those sketches." Realizing this was going nowhere, I shook my head and held out my palms. "Never mind about all that. I was being sincere. Having a Wild Hunt authority in the house is a plus."

"Indeed."

As WAS USUAL I came through the rear of the house after my morning walk with dogs bounding and nipping at each other joyfully. My cheeks were rosy enough that I could pass for pure Irish.

"Keir!" I called as I hung up my wax coat and traded the Wellies for Ugg slip-ons.

"Lair!"

I heard him answer from his room. He'd picked up my joke about calling his room the 'lair' and begun using it describe the sports den as such.

He looked up when I arrived at his doorway and smiled. "You look so kissable when you're rosy."

"And yet you're still sitting in your chair," I retorted.

Feeling invigorated, I dashed away and gave a feeble, mock chase through the kitchen, where Olivia was trying to remove chocolate croissants from the oven, through the living room, but was caught up in a bear hug and carried the rest of the way to the bedroom. He kicked the door closed with one foot, set me down, turned me around and almost instantly rid me of the Lake Country December chill.

When he pulled back from a kiss that'd caused me to forget my name, he said, "There's a choice to be made."

"What is it?" I said breathlessly.

"We could go back to bed. Or have coffee and chocolate croissants."

It was cruel, I tell you. Offering a woman a choice between lovemaking with a walking fantasy in a warm bed with real linen sheets or chocolate? It was just mean.

"Ugh!" I said. "Raincheck until Olivia's gone for the day." I could tell by his semi-pout he'd hoped for choice number one. I wiggled my eyebrows. "I'm much more uninhibited when I know we have the house to ourselves."

The suggestion of naughty behavior instantly restored his good mood.

"Chocolate it is then! Not a bad consolation prize. The smell of fresh pastry was driving me mad."

Olivia politely made herself scarce and went off to attend to other rooms while we indulged in the kind of decadent breakfast dreams are made of.

"The only thing that could make this better is bacon," he said.

"Bacon?"

I blinked.

He nodded.

I shook my head.

"Bacon doesn't go with chocolate croissants. Bacon goes with eggs and biscuits. The American kind of biscuits," I added for clarification.

"Remember what you said to Esmerelda about judging what others eat?"

"No. What did I say?"

"You said, 'Are you the food police'?"

"Do you remember everything I say?"

"Yes."

I could tell that he wasn't joking.

"Yikes. I'm going to have to be more careful." His only response was to bite off half of a huge croissant. Being familiar with Keir's appetite, Olivia had made a pile of them. "But you're right. You're entitled to eat what you want. If you like bacon and chocolate together, who am I to say no?"

With a smile and a mouthful of croissant, he rose, walked to the refrigerator, retrieved a container of bacon made the day before, and returned to the table with it. With a flourish worthy of a theatrical troupe, he opened the container and proceeded to chow down with bacon in one hand and croissant in the other.

After swallowing, he said, "Sweets are lovely." He let his eyes drift downward suggestively. "But I need *meat*."

The look in his eyes made my breath catch at the same time all semblance of intelligent thought fled. I wanted to counter with a reply worthy of a siren, but instead I said, "Good to know."

Keir chuckled. He was far too amused that I'm inept at games of seduction. It's hardly fair that he's had hundreds, correction, thousands of years more time to practice sexy comebacks.

I sighed. "You win."

"Good for me. What have I won?"

"The title of wittiest person in this kitchen at this moment."

"I could die happy with an honor such as this."

"If you're looking to add funniest to the prize, you'll have to do better."

"There's nothing funny about bacon. Bacon is a very serious matter and I take it very seriously."

"Keir. Nobody could take cold, day-old bacon seriously."

"Oh contraire. It may even be better on the second day."

"That's hard to imagine."

"Try it." He held out a piece of stiff, on the well-done side, bacon.

"No thanks. I'm content with my meatless breakfast."

"Your loss." He shrugged. "What's on the schedule for today?"

"The Wild Hunt." He stopped chewing and blinked.

"No. No. I don't mean there will be one. Or that *I'm* going along. I mean Lochlan says the cloaking magic has been lifted. I can now read and remember. At least in theory. I guess I won't know for sure until I get into it."

"Hmmm." He returned his attention to the serious business of bacon.

"He says you'll be a good resource if I have questions. Are you going to be around today?"

"Mostly." I thought I heard an uncharacteristic hint of caution in that. "Do you need me to be?"

"No. Questions can wait if you have something to do." I lowered my voice. "Did you forget about choice number two?"

"Certainly not! When Rita is available and willing, I have nothing more pressing. It's a policy on which you can depend."

"Makes me feel powerful."

He laughed softly. "You have no idea, love."

I'D PROMISED MYSELF that I'd read through the very last folder on the Solstice Court pile before diving into the Wild Hunt. So I settled into the comfy chair at my library desk that felt like it was molded to fit my derriere and did just that.

The case was being brought by the Bureau of Behavioral Oversight and it was a doozy. Interspecies abuse.

A fae merchant had, at some point, decided it would be a good idea to create a perverse sort of aquarium populated by magical sea creatures. He reasoned that fae who are not able to breathe underwater would never see these varieties of magic kind otherwise. So, he'd been capturing a collection of creatures for his enterprise who would not do well imprisoned. Or on display for entertainment.

I placed that last brief on the DEFINITELY pile with a Post-it note reminder to tell Lochlan the following morning. Just in time. My deadline for docket decisions was expiring the next day. Procrastination be praised.

There was no externally initiated requirement that I understand the Wild Hunt before court week began, but I had a sense that I'd be better able to perform the solemn duties of magistrate with a grasp of the concept. I could've found truckloads of references penned by humans, but knew that path would be fruitless. I'd learned that human accounts of everything about magic and magic kind were resplendent with half-truths and outright misunderstandings.

Fetching the big book from the safe felt like my reward for completing the dockert. I opened it and pulled one of the lamps closer. I wouldn't want it widely known, but often, half the fun of the big book was the pictures, hand drawn, hand colored works of art. Illuminated like the *Book of Kells*.

Not this time.

When I arrived at the pages marked Wild Hunt, I found illustrations that were shocking. I know it's not chic or modern to admit capacity for shock, but I was still clinging to scant tatters of innocence as if my happiness depended on it.

I was positive I'd never seen those pictures before, but I supposed that memory block thing had worked well. It occurred to me that I might have relived the process I'd just gone through over and over again. I had no way of knowing.

Wild Hunt for *Groundhog Day*.

I wasn't entirely sure that I didn't want to retreat to

not remembering what I saw. The pictures depicted a teeming mass of unrelated creatures, some clothed, some half-clothed, some wearing nothing at all. They were apparently ungrounded by earth, as if they'd been simultaneously swept up into a tornado. I kept blinking, looking away, then back again, certain my mind was playing tricks because every second or two the illustration seemed to move on the page and rearrange itself slightly. Like a stop-motion video.

It was unnerving. To say the least.

For a time I couldn't pull myself away to continue reading. I was mesmerized by the depictions, frozen in a tug of war between horror and waiting to see what they'd do next. All the while I was caught up in an inner struggle, I was hoping like Hades the figures wouldn't leap from the page and come to life. Geoffrey could do it.

I've learned that, when it comes to magic, there's no way to prepare for what happens next. Because the thing I'm prepared for will *not* be what's coming. It's a perverse kind of cosmic rule.

I thought about slamming the book shut and running from the house, but instead began chanting *big girl pants, big girl pants, big girl pants.* I consciously began using meditation techniques to slow my breathing and, for once, I was grateful for the classes Evie gave me for Mother's Day when she was fifteen.

Maybe she'd meant it as a hysterical-Mom joke. Or maybe she was aware, on some level, that her mom wasn't happy. To everyone's surprise, I took the classes. If that would help me deal with this, it was worth it.

After a couple of minutes my breathing did slow and perhaps my heartrate as well. I remembered the words of one of my yoga instructors that had come and gone over the years, "Wherever you are is where you're supposed to be."

Coming to the conclusion that the only way forward was to trick myself, I improvised by gathering a couple of pieces of paper and placed them on top of the illustrations so that I could force myself to concentrate on the words.

After an hour or so of reading. I almost thought I had more questions than answers. Even with my newly acquired ability to retain what I was reading, it felt like there were gaping holes in the information. Like there was an assumption that anyone reading, and remembering, would have a certain foundation of understanding.

I'd managed to piece together that the Wild Hunt is a multipurpose event, kind of a one-stop-shop for revelry, cleaning house, and letting the dogs out. If that sounds like an unlikely combination, well, what can I tell you? I couldn't make this stuff up.

If you believe I'm making light of my initial impression, you'd be right. I'm bringing humor to bear on my attempt to stay grounded. Because I'm afraid some of this might be beyond my ability to process. It was probably wise that the Hunt had been given the magical equivalent of XXX and hidden from human view.

Here's my unclarified, unverified understanding after first pass.

The timing of the event spontaneous, but not random. It occurs at times and for reasons understood by magic kind, but not me.

A Wild Hunt is initiated by a trio of astral-traveling witches. They wake the figure currently serving as head huntsman, in this incarnation that would be Diarmuid. It's not the least surprising to learn that, in medieval times, the leader of the Wild Hunt was thought to be the "Devil", himself.

The leader calls forth his one-of-a-kind chariot drawn by a pair of black horses with horns that resemble spiked antlers. The witches then begin a chant that gives the power of flight to both chariot and horses. As the witches chant faster and faster, they create a vortex that begins to spin. As it turns faster and faster, it rises in the air and begins to fly over the earth, calling creatures throughout the fae world to join in.

As the visions unfolded, I began to see the Wild Hunt leader as the supreme rock star of fae supported by three backup singers. I wouldn't share this bit of irreverence with anyone but Keir, but it helped me keep hold of my tenuous connection to a reality I could tolerate.

The power of the Hunt's centrifugal vortex builds on itself, eventually creating its own accelerated jet stream. The willing are more or less sucked up into the mass, the same way a tornado lifts objects from the ground, until it becomes what appears to be a flying hoard of misfits.

Imagine three unrelated groups. The warlike fae, who were always down for serious partying. Horrific monsters, who are only set free by the Hunt and only remain free for the duration of the Hunt.

Last is the dead. Specifically, human dead, aka ghosts; those who did not move along to the next experience when encouraged to do so by death of the body.

These were the recalcitrant departed who did not depart because of fear of consequences for their misdeeds and/or malignance of spirit. Phantoms who fear cosmic consequences sometimes choose the hellish existence of haunting the earth over facing judgment. If they happen to be out and about on the occasion of a Hunt, they may be *in*voluntarily swept up in the whirlwind as it passes over.

In effect, the Hunt is its own kind of judgment. At some point, as the gale force air current carries them along helplessly, their ability to adhere to the collective gives way because, unlike magic kind, these spiritual residues of people, are subject to Newton's mechanics. In a process frequently misidentified as centrifugal force, they're flung away into a black hole of abyss, where they will simply cease to exist in any form. Forever.

I wasn't able to determine how long the Hunt lasts, but it was clear that it takes place in the dead of night and must be concluded before daylight, something about alerts of approaching day being sounded by three special, early-warning roosters: black, red, and white. The aspect of color coding was unclear and perhaps unnecessary. Hard to say.

After completing the reading, I moved the blank pages I'd placed on top of the pictures and looked again thinking things might seem different through the filter of newly gained insight. I wish I could say the images were less disturbing, but I can't. I replaced the book in the safe, gave each of the dogs a pet, more to comfort me than to settle them, then did my slipper shuffle through the house to find Keir.

He was settled in the furthest reclining position of his huge, leather recliner in front of his wall of screens, and looked like he was in sports heaven.

"My favorite visitor," he said when he noticed that I'd arrived at his threshold. I stood there wordlessly. He sat up and used the remote to mute the sound. "Is something wrong?"

I inhaled deeply hating how often he felt the need to ask that question.

"I'm not sure." I think I hated that answer even more.

Way to be decisive, Rita.

"Come here," he said. He opened his arms and gestured for me to curl up in his lap.

Part of me craved that. The other part felt like I couldn't relax until I had some answers.

"I can't curl up and get comfy until I've sorted out this stuff about the Wild Hunt."

"Oh," he said. Simply.

"I have questions."

He sighed. "Do you want to talk in here?"

"Um." I fiddled with the hem of my shirt.

"Let's put on a kettle. Kitchens were made for talking."

I nodded.

I took the chair closest to the kitchen fire, pulled my knees up, wrapped my arms around them, and watched as he set the kettle on the stove.

He pulled a chair directly in front of me, sat close, and rested his hands on my feet. "Now what has you all worried and drawn up into a pink ball?"

For clarification, he said that because I was wearing a pink French terry shirt and pants.

"The monsters for one thing."

He nodded. "These are things humans don't often see."

"Thank goodness. That sentence you just said? It should always be punctuated with *thank goodness.*"

He chuckled. "If you wish. You know there are ghastly things in the human world as well."

"Like what?"

"Insects with multiple sets of eyes. Crocodiles. Moray eels."

"Okay. You're right."

"If you took a person who'd never been to your reality and showed them the ugliest specimens…"

"They'd either be running back to their own world or they'd be sitting in their kitchen. Like this." I pulled my knees closer to my chest as if that would protect me from what I'd learned about the Wild Hunt.

He nodded once. "High probability."

"Alright. You make a good point. Now for the really hard stuff. Have you been on Wild Hunts?"

He tapped my toes that were hanging off the chair seat with the tips of his fingers and looked pensive. "I'd rather not say."

"Why not?"

"Because judging from your tone I believe you might think less of me if I say yes."

"Think less of you? And why's that? Because of the mid-air orgies, the interspecies copulation, or the strong suggestion that some of these bizarre couplings are rapes?"

"It's not what you think."

"It's not?" I'd intended to remain perfectly calm, but was feeling a dangerous combination of anger, confusion, and disillusionment building. His answer sounded a lot like confirmation. "Okay. I'm perfectly calm and I'm listening. Explain."

"It doesn't sound like you're calm much less perfectly. And listening with an open mind is just not happening right now. Saying it doesn't make it so."

"I'm listening with the only mind I've got."

The train engine tea kettle chose that moment to pull out of the station. Normally, I loved hearing the choo choo sound accompanied by the racket of mechanical wheels turning. But at that moment, it was an annoyance that ramped my discomfort even higher.

"Just a minute," Keir said. "Let me pour you a cup."

VICTORIA DANANN

As he walked toward the stove, I said, "You'd better give me decaf."

Under some circumstances that might've been a joke. On this occasion it was a preemptive measure to keep my temper in check. Emotional escalation was a looming possibility.

When Keir was reseated and both of us had cups in hand, which did lend a cloak of civility to a conversation about the antithesis of civilization. I suppose I'd known all along there was a reason why the Hunt was called "wild" and not fun, or invigorating, or educational.

As the silence expanded, I was first to blink. "Talk."

"Trying to decide what to say."

"If you're having to choose words *that* carefully, it's a tip off that something's wrong."

That utterance was the kind of déjà vu moment most parents who've survived teenagers can relate to. And I *hated* sounding like a parent with my lover.

"Well, that's the crux, isn't it? What's 'wrong' to you isn't necessary 'wrong' to everyone else. Particularly not magic kind. With a few exceptions, human cultures are different as they logically would be.

"Species such as ourselves, who frequently live as long as we choose, and only procreate when we choose, experienced a cultural evolution that's very different in character. We have no need to form family units that double as economic units or anything of the sort."

I *hated* granting quarter, even a little, but I was following his explanation thus far.

"There are some who join the Hunts who…" He paused and looked away as if my understanding depended on the next thing he said. He sighed. "This is hard to explain. But they consent to nonconsensual fornication."

"I can see why that would be hard to explain."

"There are those, not many, but some, who find gratification in pretending to rape. Or be raped. The Hunts satisfy those appetites so that they remain in check." He poured a splash of cream into his cup and said, "Kind of like your, ah, Mardi Gras."

It would have been nice to call that ridiculous, but as I mulled it over I realized it made too much sense to discount out of hand. I fully understood the point underlying masks and crowds and dates designated to satisfy prurient impulses. Permission for excess to the obscene immediately precedes a religious demand for personal sacrifice.

"Play-acting?" He nodded. "And these miscreants know how to recognize each other? So no one who hasn't consented to non-consent gets accidentally, um, tagged?"

He nodded again, more emphatically. "Right. Absolutely right."

I studied his beautiful face for a few seconds. He was solemn, clearly worried, and unless Esme was lying about my budding intuition, sincere.

"I have to assume, because of your answer earlier, that you've, um, been on Hunts before."

"I'm fairly certain that all magic kind have experienced a Hunt." I somehow knew this statement was about to be followed with a comparison to something human. "Just as most humans have been to a big venue music concert. From our point of view, meaning magic kind, the Hunt performs a service that maintains balance for both fae and humans."

"You mean because it's a ghost sweep?"

He frowned momentarily before realizing what I meant. "That's part of it. Yes. There would definitely be a surplus of unpleasant spooks if not for the Hunts."

I drank from my cup and stared into it for a while, processing Keir's words as I swirled the liquid around. It was a point of view worth considering. And, I reminded myself, my personal cultural norms weren't universal. There was scandalous behavior, by my standards, afoot amid humanity as well.

When I raised my eyes to meet his, he said, "No."

"I'm going to need more."

"No. I'm not one of those who enjoys acting out rape while in the middle of a flying tumbler filled with bodies. It does not buzz my tittilater."

When I almost laughed, I realized that I had relaxed considerably and might be coming to terms with the fact that such things as Wild Hunts exist. After all, I'd come to terms with the fact that sadomasochistic dens exist for humans whose twisted psyches prompted seriously aberrant behavior.

But there was a big distinction.

I didn't know any den masters. Or Mardi Gras kings.

But I knew Diarmuid.

"What does?" I blurted.

His smile was accompanied by the twinkle I was so fond of. "Beautiful, smart, funny Americans with mahogany hair, multihued eyes, and good chat."

And just like that, I set my puritanical misgivings about the Wild Hunt aside.

"Make that singular and I'll give you the last chocolate croissant."

"Done. What gets my engine going is a beautiful, smart funny American with mahogany hair, multihued eyes, good chat, and a movie star name."

I grinned. "That sounds like me."

He chuckled. "Right you are. Where's my croissant?"

CHAPTER FIVE

Jet Planes and Jingle Bells

IT WAS THE Saturday afternoon of John David's holiday party. He was still planning an Imbolc masked ball, but apparently had decided he liked throwing parties so much that he couldn't get enough of it. That was more than agreeable to the other locals, who'd responded by accepting him as an insider.

I was beyond pleased that I'd finished evaluating the piles and piles of potential cases so that Lochlan could finalize the docket before the Solstice Court Meet commenced on Monday morning. I had two days with nothing to do but enjoy the season and have a good time.

It was hours before I needed to get ready, but I set out the dress I planned to wear. It was ordered online, but looked like it had been made for me. A body-hugging, full length, red silk with high neck, long sleeves, small discreet shoulder pads for a look of impeccable tailoring and vertical rows of tiny beads. Not enough to make it heavy or tacky. Just enough to catch the light whenever I moved. It was glamorous enough to be worthy of the original Rita Hayworth.

I was expecting Lily when the doorbell rang. I'd asked her to create a spectacular Yule wreath for me to take to John David as a host gift. You know, something for the vampire who has *everything*.

When I opened the door, I saw that she'd outdone herself. Pixies are rather literal. If you use a word like 'spectacular', they think you mean it. The wreath had a foundation of pine needles and cones with magnolia and grape leaves woven into the mix. Lily had then mixed in red roses, white lilies, holly with red berries, and scant tufts of mistletoe for the perfect accent. Like the cherry on top.

"Lily!" I gushed. "It's the most beautiful wreath ever created."

She giggled. "Was fun making it," she said, handing it over as she stepped inside. "It will last until the first of the year, inside or out. If he hangs it on his front door, the flowers will be fine. They're on little spell sticks that will keep them at perfect temperature in any weather."

I looked at the flowers. "That's... incredible. If I could get the patent for that and sell to humans, I'd be mega rich."

She laughed. "You're already mega rich. It's normally an extra charge, but of course, for you it's a gift."

My eyes jerked to hers and I caught the mischievous gleam. My Hallow Hill neighbors were always trying to get me to slip up and accept a gift, which was taboo for the magistrate.

"It's no such thing and you know it." I laughed. "Send the bill to Maggie."

"Oh. Alright." She pretended to be disappointed.

"So, I'll see you later? At John David's?"

"How could you possibly keep *anybody* away from a party at John David's? It's even better than lunch at your house." She almost gasped when she realized where her chatter had led. "I didn't mean... You know your lunches are just the best thing..."

I chuckled. "Lily. Stop. I happen to agree with you.

John David's parties are the Hallow Hill social events of every season."

She grinned. "What do you think he has in store for you this time?"

"It had better be food, wine, good company, maybe music, and *no* surprises." She chuckled. "I grilled him until I was satisfied that there'd be no surprises."

"Very well," she said.

"I believe him. If he lied to me, I'll take this wreath right back."

"I'm sure he's good for his word. After all you're his oldest living friend."

I guessed she meant that I was first local to make friends with him and that all the people who'd been his friends when he was alive were long since passed.

"Are you bringing a date?" I teased.

"As a matter of fact, I am." I hadn't expected that answer. "A cousin of Lochlan's who's visiting."

"Really? I haven't seen any strangers coming or going."

For heaven's sake. I sounded exactly like what's always said about small town life; that I knew everybody else's business and secretly spied on my neighbors.

She shrugged. "Well, you'll meet him later then." She looked over her shoulder toward Lochlan's and Ivy's house. "Don't tell, but he's cuter than Lochlan. Funnier, too."

I didn't have the heart to tell her that everybody was funnier than Lochlan. He had an encyclopedic list of assets, but humor wasn't one of them. On the one hand it was surprising to hear the hint of a little sibling rivalry. On the other, it seemed like the most natural thing in *any* world.

"What are you wearing?" I changed the subject in the style of magic kind.

"Green." She turned and opened the door. "Must be on my way so I can close up and get ready."

"Thank you for this." I raised the wreath hanging from my arm a few inches as if there might be a question about what was meant. "I'm going to love giving it to him."

"Anytime," she said as she stepped off the porch.

I closed the door and was deciding on the best place to store the wreath until time to go, when the doorbell rang again. Naturally, I thought Lily had forgotten something.

I swung the door wide saying, "What did you…?"

The words froze in mid-sentence. It wasn't just that words were frozen in my mouth. All thought was frozen in my brain as well. There stood my daughter, who was scheduled to arrive the *following* Saturday. *After* court meet.

"Mom!" She gave a tiny jump, an excited squeal, and rushed forward for a hug. I swung the wreath out of harm's way just in time to keep it from being crushed by enthusiasm. "Can you believe it? I'm here a WEEK EARLY!"

"Um. No. I really can't believe it."

When the ability to think did return, it arrived on a gush of every bad word I've ever heard, internally drilled like rapid fire, staccato curses.

"Oh. Who's this? Oh my god! Mom, you have dogs!"

The two, ahem, Border Collies were practically turn-ing cartwheels trying to get her attention. She was just as delighted by them as they were by her. One hurdle down.

After recognizing each dog with a round of petting, she said, "So, I was able to convince every professor to let me take finals early because, you know, they like me. Since the ticket was first class, no additional fees. Sweet, right? Oh my god! First class is unbelievable! I can't wait to tell you all about the trip.

"And this little village where you live? Is there a place on earth more picturesque? It looks like a postcard come to life. No wonder you don't want to come home. Who would?" She took a breath but didn't let up. "And this house! Could it be more charming? The answer is no. It looks like a fairytale.

"Dad and his girlfriend…" She decided not to finish that sentence. With another little jump she said, "I have to see the rest of the house and can't wait a second longer."

I didn't stand a chance of mounting a protest before she rushed past me. Keir stepped into the living room to see what was going on. She rushed past him, but said, "Oh. Hi," on her way to the bedroom.

There I was with a wreath on my arm and the front door standing wide open while the sephalian gave me a curious look.

"Evie?" he mouthed silently.

I nodded mutely knowing every bit of color had drained from my face.

When she reappeared in the living room, she'd gone from doing an impression of the circus come to town to being quiet as the grave. She looked from me to Keir and back again.

"You have two closets."

I nodded. "That's right."

She looked at Keir. "One of them is full of men's clothing."

I nodded again. "That's right, as well."

Feeling the chill on the backs of my leggings, I decided it was time to close the door. After doing so, I said, "Let me find a place for this. It's a gift for a friend who's hosting a holiday party tonight. If I'd known you were coming…"

She held up her hand. "Of course, you're right. I shouldn't have done the surprise thing. I just thought…" I watched her expression change as it seemed to dawn on her for the first time that a surprise might not be well-received. Since nothing was more important to me than her happiness, I couldn't stand the look of uncertainty that had replaced ecstasy.

"There won't ever be a time when you're not welcome,

Evie. Surprise or not," I rushed to say. "Keir. I think she left a bag standing on the porch."

He nodded and started for the door. While he did so, I hurried to the kitchen, hung the wreath from a pot rack hook, looked through the kitchen window and said, "Evangeline."

Glory be and thank you Maeve, the guest cottage sprung into being looking as if it had been sitting there all along.

I opened the mudroom door and hurried down the flagstone walk to open the cottage. After opening the door, I said, "Lights. Fire."

Keir was close behind with my daughter and her bag, but I'd beat them to it.

"Evie," I said, "the guest cottage is yours." She looked around noncommittally. "Why don't you get situated? Then come to the kitchen for some tea and a snack?"

Keir stood the bag in her bedroom.

She glanced at Keir before looking my way. "And some straight talk?"

"Sure. I'm as much about straight talk as you are. How many boyfriends did you say you'd had since Harrison?"

Her face went slack.

That was okay. I thought it best to establish some ground rules. She was the almost-graduate student who'd been brought into the world by me, raised by me, and was still being supported by me. I was the adult with every right to live my life without consulting her. She was the kid who had no right to have an opinion about my choices.

Her attitude had struck a nerve and I was on a roll. "This," I pointed at Keir, "is Keir Culain. He's the love of my life and I'd never have found him if your father hadn't dumped me. So, for that I'm grateful to your dad. And his girlfriend. May her happiness rest in peace." That last part was a little catty. I should have quit sooner, but like I said, rolling like a river.

When I looked at Keir, he blinked twice and I realized it probably wasn't the optimal scenario for revealing my feelings and making a dramatic pronouncement of love. His smile grew slowly just before he eased out of the cottage to give us some space.

Evie was quiet. Unusual, but good. It meant she was thinking about the fact that maybe her mother wasn't on earth *solely* to serve and support her.

I took a deep breath. "Let's start over. I wasn't expecting you. Okay. So, you surprised me. I love you and I'm glad you're here. I had this cottage built for your visits. I hope you like it." She looked around. "When you're settled in, come to the kitchen for tea. No need to knock. We'll be expecting you."

She didn't need me to draw attention to that last sentence with verbal machinations. She was a smart girl.

I practically ran back to the house.

"Keir!" I said breathlessly.

"Right here." He sat by the kitchen fire and his calm was a soothing balm to my frazzled nerves.

"I need a favor."

"You want me to leave."

I scowled. "No. I do not want anything of the sort. I want you to keep her occupied while I run an errand."

"Occupied? Like babysitting?" His eyebrows shot up.

"Well… Sort of."

"Are you going to offer some suggestions as to how I do that? Movies? Scrabble? Baking? Tales of the Wild Hunt?"

"This is not a time for jokes, Keir."

"But you'll forgive me anything. You know why?"

"Why?"

He grinned. "Because I'm the love of your life."

"Can we have that talk another time? There's an emer-gency afoot."

"Very well. How do I do this?"

"You're good at conversation. Make some tea and ask questions. Everybody likes talking about themselves."

"So I don't have to physically restrain her."

I gaped. "No, Enforcer. That won't be necessary. Use your charm. And your wit."

"How long are you going to be gone?"

"Um. Half an hour?"

"Alright. I don't think I have more than a half hour's charm and wit."

I started to go then stopped. "And don't let her leave."

"Don't let her leave? You just said…"

"No!" I waved a hand in the air. "Be creative. You're creative."

"I'm not."

"Of course, you are. Remember when you sawed off

the bottom piece of firewood that was preventing the door from closing?"

"Rita. That's not creativity."

"What is it then?"

"Problem solving?"

"We have a winner. If the occasion arises, problem solve."

He sighed. I left before he had a chance to think of the thousand and one reasons why I shouldn't be putting him in that position.

I ran across the lane to Lochlan's, banged on the door and felt a huge wave of relief when he opened up.

"Lochlan! It's an emergency. I need everybody in town to meet me at Molly's right now!"

"What?"

"I can't stop. Help me get everybody there."

He nodded.

I took off at a run.

I made the same speech to Braden, Maggie and Dolan, Esme, Lily on my way to the pub and finally Molly when I arrived. Fie happened to be there. Within minutes everyone else had arrived.

"Good scramble," I announced breathlessly.

"Bloody Beggars Balls, Rita," Maggie scolded. "A fine time for a fuss. Just hours before the vampire's party."

"I know. I know. It can't be helped. My daughter just showed up on my doorstep." Pause. "As a surprise." Pause. "A WEEK EARLY!"

I knew I was sounding hysterical, but I was in dire need of shared panic.

After a stunned silence, Maggie said, "Well. There's only one thing to be done." Every head in the room swiveled to look at her like she was E.F. Hutton. "We will share everything with her for the course of her stay and have a traveler wipe her memory of the visit just as she's settin' off."

Out of all the questions I might have posed, and there were many, I lit on, "What's a traveler?"

"'Tis a specialist who goes about providin' a needed service. Such as erasin' from a human's mind somethin' 'twould no' be in our best interest for them to know."

I could tell by the nods of heads and murmurs of ascent that the idea was gaining traction.

"And it's a hundred percent guaranteed to cause no

harm?"

Maggie looked around. "I ne'er heard tell of a negative side effect."

I looked at Lochlan. "Do you agree this is the best way forward?"

"I believe I do. Simple. Easy. Straightforward. And, as Margaret said, there's no harm. For the Yule holiday, your Evie can share your life, know what you know, then go home with a pleasant memory of a stay in a quaint human town."

"The court meet?" I asked.

"We can arrange for her to spend the time in tourist pursuits if she wishes. Or she can attend," Lochlan answered.

"Attend? The court meet? With me in the role of magistrate?"

There was a part of me that was excited for her to see what dear old mum was really up to and part of me that was horrified she'd find out that we share a world with magic kind and what *they're* up to.

"Well. You are the magistrate. You don't just play one on TV," Fie wisecracked.

I blinked. "What about John David's party?"

Lochlan clapped his hands together. "What better introduction? We'll all be there. We can share the nature of your new life."

"And keep her locked away until she stops screaming," Esmerelda added.

I gave Esme a look. "You know that's not funny, right?" The fact that Esmerelda didn't say she never jokes, which is her typical response to my query about being funny, she gave up nothing but a tiny smile. "Very well. If you're going to be tightlipped, I'm going to put that in the joking column."

I looked around. "You all think this is the best idea?" Everyone responded with agreement. "If she chooses to go running around the countryside during court week instead of attending, aren't you worried that she might be eager to tell others what she sees and hears?"

"Will ye no' be askin' her to keep it under her hat?" Maggie said.

"Well… yes. I will be asking that."

"And do ye no' trust her?"

Did I trust her? That was such a good question, spoken by someone who'd never been a parent. The issue of trust and parenting was complicated. What you want most in the world is to trust your offspring. But ofttimes a history of deceit on subjects ranging from missing cookies and crayon on the wall to illicit parties gets in the way of that.

We'd had our moments when Evie'd been a teen when she'd made valiant efforts to get away with this and that. At times she'd proved to be a convincing liar. But she was much younger then. In the end I said, "I think so," not so much because I did, but because I didn't want my friends to think badly of her. Nor did I want them to judge me harshly for my failures as a mom.

"Well, there ye have it," Maggie said as if the matter was decided and closed. "Ye best be callin' the vampire to let him know there'll be one more for dinner."

I sighed. "In for a penny, in for a pound?"

"All for one. One for all," Braden said gamely.

So I proceeded to get my priorities in order. "She's going to need a dress for tonight. Who has an evening gown fit for a twenty-three-year-old? Size ten."

I looked pointedly at Esme, who rolled her eyes. "Perhaps." She looked at her nails. "It will cost you."

"Of course." To the rest of the party, I said, "Thank you for coming on such short notice. I feel like we're in a conspiracy together for the duration of December. Thank you for that as well. I'd better get back. Keir is trying to keep her occupied."

While everyone was making their way toward the door, I pulled my phone from the pocket of my puffy sweater and dialed John David.

"Hello?"

"Oh, good. I'm so glad you answered," I said.

"Glad I answered? Isn't that why you called? Because you were expecting me to answer?"

"J.D. I don't have time for word games right now. I'm in a pickle and need to ask a favor. Is it alright if we bring one more for dinner?"

"Of course. Just make sure she's young, beautiful and tasty."

That would probably have been funny under any other circumstances, but in this case, it was in the worst of taste. And I could've kicked myself for the pun as soon as I thought it.

"That would have been a bloody, beastly thing to say under the best of circumstances. But since it's my daughter we're talking about, I insist you apologize. Right now."

"I withdraw the remark. Of course."

That was good enough. "No funny business tonight. My nerves are probably going to be on a hair trigger. It's turned into a coming out party. All our friends are going to reveal their true natures to my human child."

"It would be untoward for me to mention the potential of entertainment in that, wouldn't it?"

"It would. Just please. Be on your best behavior. She doesn't know vampires are real."

"I'll do my best impression of a gentleman."

"That's all I can ask. Thank you. And no pretending to eat people."

"Not tonight."

"Promise."

"Yes. Promise."

"Okay. I have a present for you. I can't wait for you to see it!"

"A present?"

He sounded so excited I was glad I'd thought to take a

gift.

I JOGGED HOME. When the door opened ahead of my arrival, I ran straight in and heard light laughter coming from the kitchen. The sound made me close my eyes from relief that things had gone okay at home.

"I'm home!" I called.

"Back here," Keir answered, even though we both knew that I knew where they were.

When I arrived on the scene, Evie was smiling, a cup of hot chocolate with little marshmallows sitting on the table in front of her. I felt of rush of warm fuzzies run through my blood stream accompanying the flash memory of times when it was so gratifying to be some-body's mother. Nurturer in chief.

"Did you know you have a car in your kitchen?" she said. It was a silly question, but it was obvious that she intended it to be. "I mean, if a person was going to have a car in their kitchen, that would be a stellar choice. An Alpha Romeo, Mom? Just how much money did we come into?"

There was the 'we' again.

I gave Keir a look that I hoped conveyed all the gratitude I felt.

Deliberately sidestepping the question about finances, I said, "Technically Romeo is not *in* the kitchen. He's in his stall. He has his own room adjacent to the kitchen so that he can be part of things. But it is separate. Sort of."

"Be part of things?" She asked.

Two tiny scowl lines tried to form between her brows, but her skin was so young and perfect that I knew they'd disappear like magic as soon as she released the tension.

I'd grown too comfortable saying things that would get me tested for dementia in the human world. Of course, Evie would expect an explanation as to why I thought Romeo would be lonely if left in a dark garage by himself. Actually, since Romeo was not magical in any way, I'd have a hard time making that explanation to anyone, human or fae. It was a matter to be taken up with my rational self as time permitted.

Turning my attention to the muddle at hand, I said, ""Guess what?"

I was hoping my tone conveyed enough excitement to raise both curiosity and anticipation.

"What?" Evie took the bait. *Good girl.*

"You're going to the party tonight! With us!" Keir's eyes widened and I knew he was thinking I was past daft, all the way to barmy. We'd grown close enough that I could guess his thoughts in Brit-speak. "All our friends will be there and are dying to meet you. I'm having a dress delivered for you in a little while. You'll have to borrow a pair of shoes from me."

"A dress?" Her question sounded like a combination of being unsure what it was and being very sure that, if I picked it out, she wanted nothing to do with it.

"Yes. Won't it be fun to glam up for a night?"

"Glam up? Who are you?"

"Somebody who's having a good time. Just like you're going to do while you're here."

"Well." She looked at Keir. "Okay." The doorbell rang. "What in the name of all that's holy was that?" she asked.

"You don't like my doorbell?"

"*That's* your doorbell?"

"What's important is that it's probably your dress!"

In my head I heard five, four, three... She scrambled up and practically ran for the front door. Some things don't change. I still know my kid.

I smiled at Keir, who still looked bowled over by the news that she was going to the party. "I'll explain in a little bit when she goes to get ready."

"Can't wait," he deadpanned.

I followed her to the front door. Braden stood on the other side and was talking to Evie.

"Oh. I see you've met the silversmith," I said. "Braden, it was nice of you to bring this around. Thank you."

I took the zippered bag from his grasp.

"Lovely to meet your daughter. See you later, Magistrate." The instant he said it, he knew it as a goof and his face fell.

"Yes. See you later."

Braden couldn't get away fast enough.

"Why did he call you Magistrate?" Evie asked.

"Tell you later. We've run out of time to do anything but get ready. I need a hot bath and a loofah. But first we need to see the dress and pick shoes."

I handed the bag to Evie and led her to my bedroom where she unzipped.

I should've known Esme would work her magic. It was

Evie's favorite shade of salmon, that unique color that went so well with her strawberry blonde hair and shocking blue eyes. As her mother, I thought she was the most perfect young woman ever to walk the face of the earth. Setting that aside, being purely objective, I knew she was a stunner by any standards. Striking enough to pass as a fae royal. She had the kind of beauty that was as much curse as blessing. The kind that gets a girl noticed by everybody, good *and* bad.

"Oh my God," she said, holding it up to her. It had three-quarter sleeves, a vee neck, and it looked like it would fall to shin length. "It's gorgeous. Do you think it'll fit?"

I breathed deeply knowing it would. "Guaranteed. Let's find shoes."

"There may be no need," she said. "There's a pair of shoes here in the bottom of the bag." She pulled them out. Esme was going to charge my account out the wazoo for this, but it would be worth it. The heels were covered in the same silk shantung as the dress with big rhinestone buckles and tiny rhinestone ankle straps. "I really, really, really hope these fit," she said. "Because, you know, how could shoes be better."

Yes. Esme had a gift for pairing people with the dream clothes.

"Bet they do." I walked into my closet and pulled out my long white wool coat and handed it off to her. "You're going to need this. It's chilly after dark."

She took the coat and draped it over her arm with the dress bag.

"I am looking forward to hearing all about your trip. Can I get a raincheck for breakfast in the morning?"

She brightened. "Sure."

"Excellent. I looked at my watch. Be back in an hour and a half and get ready to be wowed."

"Wowed?"

"It will be a night you'll never forget."

I could see by the sparkle in her eyes that she liked the sound of that.

"The house is wonderful, Mom. I wouldn't have thought something like this suits you, but it does. And, um, Keir."

"Yes?"

"He's great, too." She laughed. "Guess I could say the

same as about the house. I wouldn't have thought he suits you, but he does."

"Yeah."

The fact that Evie was flexible and adaptable was working in my favor. I was hoping we weren't about to throw too much Twilight Zone her way. Everybody has limits.

When she'd gone to the guesthouse, Keir ambled in and leaned against the wall, arms crossed.

"I guess you want to know what happened while I was gone?"

He chuckled. "A very good guess."

"I called for an emergency muster at the pub. What followed was a magnificent rally."

"Go on."

"Everybody showed up in minutes. I explained the problem. Quickly. And it was Maggie who came up with the solution. To quote, she said, 'There's only one thing to be done'."

"There's a conversation stopper."

"True. But there was hardly time for committees or consensus."

"Also true. And her answer was?"

"Let it all hang out then wipe her memory before she gets on the westbound plane."

He searched my eyes. "You're kidding."

"No." My pleasure in believing we'd come to the ideal solution was wavering. "You think it's a bad idea."

"Well, it doesn't really matter what I think because it's done now, isn't it?"

"Um. Yes?"

His expression softened just before he walked forward and pulled me into a hug. "It's as good a choice as any. It's not like I can think of a better plan."

I pulled back. "Thank you for keeping her occupied while I alerted everybody that we have an incoming human presence."

He chuckled. "My pleasure."

"Do you like her?"

"Like her? Of course. She's yours. How could I not like her?"

CHAPTER SIX

Jovial John

I WAS TYING Keir's bow tie, feeling like a movie star, when he said, "I think I heard a knock on the back door."

"You must have ears like a bat."

I was secretly pleased that Evie knocked and didn't come right in. I opened the door and said, "You look amazing, sweetheart."

"I thought I did until I saw you." After a head to toe scan, she said, "Wow. Your midlife disruption has been good for you."

"Yep." I nodded. There was no point in pretending that I didn't know I was better off in every way quantifiable. "Come take the coat off and let me see you."

She took the coat off and turned in a full revolution.

"What do you think?"

I could hear in her voice and tell by her manner that she was as pleased with the outfit as if she'd designed it herself. Esme was good like that.

I heard Keir walk into the kitchen just before I said, "Evie. You look like Jessica Rabbit."

Keir laughed.

Evie's smile fell and I instantly hated my big mouth for taking that self-confident ecstasy from her face.

The scowl was back. "Who's Jessica Rabbit?"

Keir laughed again. I wished I wasn't too pain averse to hit him.

It was clear that I'd disengaged the brake between brain and mouth, and the consequence was needing to scramble to put that look of happiness back on my kid's face.

"Jessica Rabbit is a cartoon character who is the epitome of voluptuous glamour."

I didn't lie. That was true. And I managed to deliver my line without a hint of judgment. Maybe being magistrate was teaching me better control. *Yay me.*

What's also true is that I liked seeing my daughter in

jeans, tees, and stylish vests. Seeing her in a dress designed to accentuate curves I didn't know she possessed was an unwanted confrontation with time and worry. First, I had to admit my daughter was close to the same age as Rita Hayworth when she was the top WWII pinup. *Geez.* That meant also admitting that I was old enough to have a daughter at the age when a woman might be known as a love goddess. *GEEZ!*

The second part of that is the worry that accompanies being the mom of *that* girl.

Jessica, I mean Evie, turned when Keir walked into the kitchen.

"Wow," she said. "You look like James Bond at Monte Carlo. Well, I mean if James didn't always opt for the clean cut Brylcreem look.

Before he could respond, I chortled. "What would you know about Brylcreem?"

"Granddad used it sometimes."

"Oh, yeah. He did."

"You both look lovely," Keir said. "And Romeo awaits."

Evie turned her head toward Romeo's stall. "Cinderella could only wish."

"That's my girl." I chuckled.

I slipped on my black ostrich feather cape, grabbed the wreath, and we were off.

"THE CAR CAN drive itself?" Evie sounded like she'd just heard about Disneyworld.

"It can, but sometimes we choose to be in control. Don't we, Keir?"

He laughed. Keir wouldn't allow Romeo to drive if both arms were broken.

I turned around so that I could see Evie in the backseat. "If you want to go exploring by yourself this week, I will make Romeo available. It's better than having a chauffeur. You just tell him where you want to go and he does everything for you."

"Woooooow," she said softly.

"It's a ticket ride."

"How far are we going?"

"From here. Ten minutes. Depending on how fast Keir feels like going."

"Who all will be there?"

"Since you don't know any of our friends and neighbors, you wouldn't know more after a list of names than you do now."

"I guess I meant how many?"

"Oh." I looked at Keir. He looked at me and shrugged. "Probably just twenty."

"Okay."

We spent the rest of the short drive discussing the disappearing experience of darkness of night in that part of the country and how it compares to Oxford.

As we entered the estate and were driving on a private road, Evie grew quiet. When the house came into view, lit like a monument to modern electricity, Evie said, "Who do you know?" in an awestruck tone.

"You remember when I tried to teach you about managing posh place settings?"

"Yeah?"

"And you blew me off saying you would never be in a situation in your life when you needed to know what to do with superfluous cutlery?" Mom I-told-you-so's are terribly unfair. Also enormously satisfying to the Mom delivering said told-you-so. "Well, sit next to me and do what I do. Where flatware is concerned," I clarified.

I LOOKED UP at the sound of the heavy door being pulled open.

"Hello, Jarvis."

John David's butler beckoned us in with a wave. "Good evening, madam."

"I'd appreciate it very much if you'd locate Mr. Weir and ask him to come to the door."

Jarvis appeared to be grappling with an unseen conflict. After what appeared to be a tortured reluctance, the man complied.

As soon as he was out of sight, Evie said, "His name's not *really* Jarvis."

"You know," I said, "I thought the same thing when I met him. Maybe domestic agencies encourage the staff in their stable to use aliases."

She was nodding. "That would make sense."

Mere seconds later John David entered the grand foyer with a wide, handsome grin, looking like black tie had been invented for him.

Evie leaned into me and whispered. "Scratch what I said about Keir and James Bond. This guy is the *real* 007."

"Rita!"

John David sounded like, in his opinion, the party didn't start until I arrived. I was sure there'd never been anyone else in my life who saw me that way. Or maybe it was because I'd told him I was bringing a present.

I held up the wreath. "For you! Happy Season!"

He stared at the wreath for a couple of seconds before saying, "It's wonderful. Thank you." It was the most, sincere sounding thankyou I'd ever received.

He recalled Jarvis, who'd stepped away to take care of our wraps, and handed off the wreath. "See that this gets affixed to the front door in customary fashion, will you?"

"Indeed. Very good, sir." Jarvis gave a single nod of the head that somehow left the impression of a full body bow.

John David turned his attention, and predatory smile, toward Evie.

"Who's this?" said the spider.

"My daughter, Evangeline." Evie elbowed me. "She goes by Evie. That's what we all call her. That's what she wants to be called by everyone. Including you."

John David's eyes had widened at the same time he scowled. "You said she was a child. I hired a nanny!"

It took a second before I grasped the misunderstanding. "I didn't say she is *a* child. I said she's *my* child. There's a big difference."

"I fail to see it," he said.

"I'm sorry I wasn't completely clear. Is there enough food?"

John David's face relaxed into smooth features and the tiniest smile. He knew that was a ridiculous question.

"Of course! That's a ridiculous question," he said.

"Would you like me to reimburse you for the expense of the nanny?" I asked.

That earned me an outright laugh. "What is the matter with me?" He turned to Evie. "Young lady. I'm delighted to have you in my home."

Evie laughed in a way that sounded far too womanly for my liking. She might not look like a little girl to others, but she was *my* little girl. *Wasn't she?*

"Young lady?!?" Her tone sprayed enough incredulity to fill the grand foyer and spill into other rooms. "How old are you?"

John David's smile fell as he took her meaning and straightened. "Old enough to be uninterested in being 'woke'."

After getting past the mortification of having my daughter be rude to our host while having literally just entered his house, I decided to settle on the bright side of their exchange. They hated each other.

Good.

I was glad they'd rubbed each other the wrong way. I hadn't liked the feeling of having a vampire look at my baby like she was a banana split.

I stepped in and took John David's arm, hoping to interrupt the awkwardness. As we walked toward the drawing room, I said, "Did everybody fill you in?"

"About everything except whether to expect a child or a woman."

I ignored the poke. "Good."

"How do you want to do it?"

I continued walking only because my legs have muscle memory. My brain had stopped dead. "Do it?"

"How do you want to tell her that her mother is the

only other human for dinner tonight?"

"*At* dinner. Not *for* dinner."

"Whatever." He smiled. "Announcement at dinner? Winged lion and pixie show?"

"I… hadn't made a plan."

"Would you like my help?"

"You could help?" It seemed the tact compartment in my brain had a leak.

"I can if you wish."

Fortunately, he hadn't heard the overarching surprise in my question. "I suppose that, if you have any plan at all, it's more than I've got."

"Very well. Consider it done."

I felt a little thrill of nonsensical pride for realizing that I'd guessed right. Counting Evie and Jeff, appearing as himself, there were exactly twenty for dinner. Lucky all around because one more person would have strained the capacity of John David's dining table. It might've meant several fewer crystal stems and pieces of silverware at each place. *Oh my!*

Moving around the room with Evie in tow, I began introducing her to the people I'd come to think of as community. We hadn't gotten very far when John David spoke up.

"Dinner is served."

John David had placed Evie at the opposite end of the table from himself. I surmised that his intention was to make her the honored guest sitting at the secondary 'head' of the table. I was seated to her left with Braden on my left. Keir was somewhere in the middle of the mix. Fie was at Evie's right with Molly on his other side.

Fie was as charming and welcoming to Evie as he'd been to me my first day in Hallow Hill. He was a good first meet. What I saw when I looked her way was what every mom wants to see when she looks at her daughter. She was relaxed and glowing like the star she was. She raved about the food, the drink, the clothes, and about John David's manor house.

"We all got a tour one day. He had us to lunch and then showed us around like we were tourists," I said.

"I'll bet that was wonderful," she said seriously. "The paintings alone…" Her tone was almost reverent.

"We might be able to arrange a private tour while you're here," I said. Leaning in conspiratorially, I stage-whispered, "I know the owner,' and winked.

Everybody laughed.

As instructed Evie surreptitiously tracked my utensil choices and mimicked them as smoothly as if she was to the manor born. *Gads.* She was good at pretense. She could've been a spy. Maybe that's why she kept mentioning James Bond.

I used these bits of mental distractions to keep my mind off the upcoming big reveal and hoped we, meaning the collective, had made the right decision. I was growing increasingly edgy wondering what John David had in mind. Remembering the judgement, or lack thereof, he'd exercised when designing a murder mystery dinner to prank me, I must've been temporarily insane to let him take charge of this mess.

That's it.

I was made temporarily insane by the sheer absurdity of the situation. I was living a secret life on the other side of Alice's looking glass and had been caught by my kid.

"Mom. Are you okay?"

Did I hear Mom?

"What?" The diners in our immediate vicinity were

staring.

After dinner, our aforenamed host invited us to join him in the drawing room for coffee and liqueur. When everyone was present and outfitted with coffee or a glass of brandy, he banged a tiny gong with a tiny hammer. Miniature gong sounds are a little comical, but it got our attention. Evie was sitting on an authentic bergère chair that had, at some point, been reupholstered in a satin stripe alternating cream and a salmon color close to the value of her dress. It looked like a lot of thought had been given to staging because she was in the best spot for a presentation. And she was a vision.

"Dearly Beloved," John David began.

Oh God. What was the freaking vampire doing now!?

"We are gathered here tonight," he continued.

Does he think he's being funny?

"To welcome our new honorary Hallow Hill resident, Evangeline."

I knew by the gleam in his eye, that he used her proper name to get her goat. It did.

"Evie," I spoke up. Everyone looked at me. "She prefers to be called Evie." When it was clear that my outburst had concluded, the guests turned their attention back to John David.

"I'm now going to turn the after-dinner education portion of the evening over to our mayor, Fie Mistral."

"Oh, for…" I heard Lochlan say and turned in time to see him get a pinch on the arm from Ivy. "Ouch. Well, he's the *unelected* mayor."

A group chortle made its way around the room.

Fie stood and said, "Yes. Lochlan is correct." He looked down at Evie. "We don't hold elections. We don't have government titles because we don't have a government. Perhaps I'm called the unelected mayor because at gatherings such as this, I often find myself in this position. He looked at Lochlan as if there was a rivalry with a point to be made.

Fie smiled at Evie. "As our generous host said, in his uniquely strange way, we've come together to celebrate the holiday season, which we would have done in any case. But our reason for merriment has grown exponentially because of the unanticipated arrival of Rita's lovely daughter, Evie."

Evie didn't look the least uncomfortable with being

the center of attention. If anything, I would say she was enjoying it.

"So, what you may not know is that Evie is embarking on the advanced study of…" He turned to her.

"Myths, fairytales, and folklore," she said proudly.

What? I thought she was involved in classical studies. Had she ever been so specific? Had I not been curious enough to ask?

"Yes. Exactly," affirmed Fie. "So, Evie, what if I told you there was proof that some of the figures and events in myths and fairytales are very much real?"

She stared at him for a few beats like she was trying to imagine where this might be going. "I guess I'd say, do you have proof?"

Fie grinned. "A very smart answer. As a matter of fact, we do have proof."

She set her dessert wine glass down on the little table to her right and folded her hands in her lap like she was queen of Hallow Hill. "Then I'd very much like to see it." Looking around the room she said, "Are you all scholars?"

Braden barked out a laugh. His fiancé stepped on his foot and the laughter was cut off abruptly.

After witnessing that exchange, Evie looked at me and said, "What is this?"

I winced a little, wanting to save her from any discomfort she might experience from learning that the myths she studies are not entirely mythical. My own initiation had been gradual, which was much more merciful and preferable to being thrown into the deep end with no prep or warning.

"Here's my plan," Fie said. "We're going to go around the room, introduce ourselves, and explain who we are. Who we really are. If you feel good about that, we'll follow with a few demonstrations. Proof if you will."

Evie looked wary and intrigued. "Okay."

"I'll begin. I'm Fie Mistral. I work at the Hallow Hill bank. I'm not human. I'm originally from a land that no longer exists. My friends here call me a wind devil, but I think of myself as an air elemental."

"I'm Maggie McHenry. I work at The Hallows, your mother's shop. Durin' the day. At night, I make calls to the households of those facin' imminent death, in my other form."

"Your other form?" Evie asked.

"Aye. I'm…"

"Banshee," Evie finished for her.

I let go of the breath I'd been holding. So far things were going better than anyone might've guessed.

As the process went on, Evie grew more and more serious. I thought her composure would break when John David talked about his life as a vampire, but she seemed to take it in stride. Outwardly.

I was the only one left.

She looked at me coolly. "What do you have to do with this, mother?"

Mother? She'd never called me *mother* in her entire life.

"I act as the judge when magic kind have disputes. The title is magistrate. The court meets for about a week eight times a year. If you'd arrived next Saturday, as planned," I said pointedly, "Solstice Court Week would've been over. We could have all pretended to be purely human for your holiday and no one would be the worse for wear."

She took in a deep breath, let it out, and repeated. "Worse for wear." Her eyes flicked around the room. "I thought you were a shopkeeper."

"I am," I said. "That's just not my only job. On Monday I'll be sitting in a courtroom that can't even be seen by humans unless they're granted special permission."

After thinking about that for a moment, she asked. "How did you get to be judge? And why would magical creatures do what you say?"

"That's a longer story," Lochlan broke in. "One which we're happy to relate once you're sure you feel comfortable with the fact that we're not human."

She nodded. "So you're prepared for me to see Keir become a giant winged lion? Ivy's going to become a tiny pixie and fly around the room?" She turned to Geoffrey and her smile went sardonic. "Perhaps best of all, Geoffrey can be anything. Okay. I'll play. Geoffrey, I'd like you to be a sixteen-foot python."

Without further encouragement, Geoffrey stood. The air around him blurred, then became liquid, and a second later the requested python was slithering toward Evie. It was so weird that she asked for that because I knew she hated snakes with a passion. She'd once joked that she wanted to live in Ireland because there are no snakes.

My Evie practically leapt from her chair and yelled,

"No!" The python, or rather Geoffrey stopped its advance. "Cute dog."

Geoffrey immediately changed into a Cairn Terrier and jumped up into her lap. While I was trying to not give that too much thought, Evie went from terrified to delighted in a second.

"Oh," she said. "Good boy."

Geoffrey wagged his tail and gave her face a lick.

"Jeff!" I said. He turned to look at me. "Get down right now!"

Jeff got down, easily shifted into his own form, had the nerve to give me a wink, and strolled over to the coffee service.

"My thinking is," Fie said, "that a person such as yourself who has made a life's work of the history of magic kind, as told by humans, would be singularly interested in a field study." She nodded dumbly. "You might see this as your lucky day. When you learned that myths and fairytales are real. At least to some extent."

Evie looked at me. "You're really a...?"

"Magistrate," I supplied. "Yes. Yes, I am. We're going to make it possible for you to observe on the condition that you not share anything you see or hear with other humans." She blinked. "Do you agree?"

She looked down at her dress. "That's how I got this dress that's the perfect color and the perfect size. It was magic."

Nodding, I pointed to Esme. "That's right. She's brilliant. And magical. And not cheap."

Esme smiled at that.

I was having a hard time gauging Evie's reaction. She was usually WYSIWYG, what you see it what you get. The fact that she was so… neutral was a concern.

Everyone, including me, waited quietly, not knowing what to do next. I looked back at Keir, who was standing behind my chair. He put a big hand on my shoulder and the touch was comforting, but I remembered that his initial reaction to the scene playing out before me was it was probably a cockeyed plan.

After a time of processing, she said spoke cautiously. "So, for the time I'm here, until the new year, I can prowl around and ask questions?"

My neighbors looked at one another and seemed to agree collectively with nods and murmurs.

"Stay away from Thomasin Cobb," Braden said.

"And Aoumeil, or whate're her real name is," Maggie said.

I chuckled. "Yes. Tomorrow I'll give her a tour of the Hallows and the town and show her which doors not to darken. It's very generous of all of you to agree to interviews." I looked at Evie. "That is what you're asking, right?" She nodded. "Thank you."

Fie clapped his hands together. "Well, now that that's settled. Let's have some brandy and gather round that beautiful piano upstairs. Keir can play and we'll sing Cole Porter songs."

I watched as Evie turned to Molly to ask, "Keir can play the piano?" That seemed to surprise her as much as anything that'd been said.

Having heard the question, Maggie broke in, "Oh, aye. We all learned that the last time we were here! We have to tell you about the prankin' we gave your mother." She laughed. "'Twas priceless I tell you."

On the way up the wide staircase that led to the music room Maggie entertained Evie with her telling of the murder mystery dinner. When Evie laughed, I relaxed completely and knew we were home free. For the remainder of December, she could move about freely and everyone, myself included, could be themselves. It was shaping up to be a fun and relaxing visit and I could see I'd be getting to know new things about my girl.

THE FOLLOWING DAY, Sunday, Evie arrived at the back door just as I was putting gingerbread pancakes on.

"Gingerbread pancakes?" Her excitement was a gift.

"Have to have holiday pancakes!"

She surprised me with a little squeeze from behind and a kiss on the cheek. "Perfect. Do we have good syrup?"

"Good syrup is in the mouth of the taster."

"Funny, Mom." She cocked her head. "Were you always funny?"

"Yes. But you didn't get the jokes."

"Huh. What are we doing today?"

"Catching up and the V.I.P tour of my shop and the town."

"Ooh. Sounds fun. Then tomorrow is court?"

"Yep. Will you call Keir?"

"No need," he said. "The bacon smell has been reeling

me in." Looking at Evie, he said, "Did you have fun at the party last night?"

She smiled. "I had its ups and downs. For somebody like me, it's a dream come true to get proof that this history I study isn't just a collection of tales, like generational layers of imagination."

I set a plate of bacon, a starter stack of pancakes, and the unplugged coffee percolator on the table and returned to the stove to flip more flapjacks. It was nice to listen to conversation between Keir and Evie as I worked.

"Now and then humans got something about us right," Keir said.

"That will be the fun of this." She was enthused. "Comparing my eyewitness and personal interviews to literary accounts and academic consensus."

"Are you going to show me your, uh, other form?"

I waited. My back turned to them.

"Probably not unless there's an incident at court while you're there," he said.

"Incident?"

Of course, she posed that question. Keir's statement seemed like it was intentionally designed to lead her there.

I dropped an oversized gingerbread pancake on my plate, feeling extra grateful that a side effect of the magistrate health plan was to keep my metabolism humming along. No matter what I did!

As I sat, Keir looked at me over the top of his coffee mug.

"Last night, we touched on the fact that both Lochlan…"

"The elf. The one who lives across the way," she said.

"Yes. Him. And Keir work for the court. Lochlan's job is similar to a clerk, but more important." I glanced at Keir. "Keir is court security."

"Enforcer," he said.

As Evie's head turned toward Keir, I gave him a warning blink. I'd deliberately chosen the word 'security' because it sounds much less alarming than 'enforcer'. And I was trying to ease her into what to expect at court gradually, making things sound as every day normal as possible.

What was I saying? Normal? Every day?

"Evie. Hallow Hill is like a little bastion in the storm. It's populated by warm, wonderful people who are loving, giving, caring and just happen to a different species. But that can't be said of the fae world at large." She looked at Keir who gave a tiny, close to imperceptible nod of confirmation, then back to me. "Some of the cases I've heard involve incredible cruelty, malignant off-the-charts narcissism, and a disregard for others that would be universally frowned upon in human culture. I think."

The fact that Evie was chewing gingerbread pancakes and swallowing them down with milk made the situation seem less stressful. She was waiting for me to go on, but there wasn't more to say at that point.

"You know, Mom, I'm not sure what you pictured when you learned that I've majored in myths, fairytales and folklore, but this body of work is resplendent with everything you just described. I'm about to embark on a *graduate* study. At *Oxford*. You didn't think I was reading the Disney version of *Snow White*, did you?"

The inflection her last sentence indicated that such a thing could not possibly be true. And yet, in my head, I was picturing the big, colorful books I'd read to her when she was a little girl. I wondered if the seeds for this passion were planted by that simple act of mothering and felt a wave of satisfaction that I might've had a part in helping her discover her highest and best purpose.

"Well…"

She laughed. "Caught you! You were seeing the Disney costumes. Probably hearing some strains of film soundtracks." Both things were true. "There are things in the history of the fantastic that, with a little massaging, are suitable for consumption by young, developing psyches. But there's also a lot that's a horror show."

Okay, so she was not going to be shocked. I almost wish I'd sought out her opinion before I took the job.

She reached for the syrup, which I had warmed up and put in a little pitcher. Olivia's standards were rubbing off on me. "These gingerbread pancakes are to die for."

"Thank you," I said then glanced at Keir.

"So." Evie bit into a piece of bacon and kept us waiting while she chewed, swallowed, and thought about what she was going to say next. "The creatures you call magic kind, sometimes you say fae but that's not the whole story I gather, act up in court when they don't get their way. Sounds pretty typical. Keir then turns into a giant winged lion and manages the situation. Right?"

"Well… Yes. Exactly."

Her very striking, very intelligent eyes locked onto mine. "How did you say you got this job?"

"It's a bit of a story. I still don't understand the whole of it, but I'll tell you everything I know."

It seemed like there'd be no better time than when the three of us were enjoying a leisurely Sunday morning brunch.

I described the package delivered to the Residence Inn and my decision to take a chance. I recounted how many times I'd been told that I was chosen by the Powers That Be and still had no idea what that meant. Only that they are never wrong.

"Your mother is too humble to describe the way in which she began her term, but she's made waves through the magical world. She's very inventive and has a masterful grasp on how to resolve things creatively, in a way that would mimic cosmic justice if it was personified in your mum."

Evie stared at Keir. "My mother? Rita, um, Hayworth?" She was still stumbling over the reclamation of my real (maiden) name.

"None other," Keir said. "If you decide to attend, you will undoubtedly be awed by her awesomeness."

"So, you're saying she's not just good with pancakes." Evie smiled. "By the way, I haven't said so. But your house is beautiful. On the inside it's totally you. On the outside it looks like a Disney fairytale."

"That's another story," Keir said. "Would you like to hear it?"

"Yeah," she answered.

"Well, the Irish fae queen was conscripted to supply housing for the magistrate. It comes with the job and must match the magistrate's needs and wishes. Queen Maeve stood over there, had a look in your mum's head, and voila. The house of her heart."

Evie looked at me. "This is a dream house, literally."

I chuckled. "Yeah. I guess so. How many people can say that?"

"None," Evie answered like it'd been a serious question. "So. You're not just special. You're a very, very big deal."

"In all the worlds only one human acts as judge of magic kind. That makes her a very, very big deal."

The pride with which Keir talked about me made me feel warm all over. I'd never been in a relationship with somebody who was proud of me or my accomplishments and bragged about me openly. It was the best kind of nice.

"I don't want you to feel obligated to visit court, Evie. Like I said, Romeo will take you anywhere you want to go."

She looked at me like I was spouting lunacy. "Are you kidding? Don't you get it? This is like the Holy Grail for somebody like me." She grinned. "Better than a lottery win."

"Better than pistachio ice cream in a chocolate waffle cone?"

"Well, no. Nothing's better than that."

We both laughed.

"I'm going to walk the dogs. You can come if you want." I started to get up but sat right back down. Hard. Like I'd gained an extra fifty. "I almost forgot. About the dogs…"

She came along wearing a pair of green duck hiking boots she found in my closet. The red ones with the faux tartan spats, meaning the spats were faux, not the tartan.

The tartan was blue, an ancient Irish hunting variation. I knew this because I looked it up when I bought a piece of clothing with a tartan feature.

We saw Lochlan in the distance. Fen and Frey whined until I chuckled. "Alright. Go on."

The two took off like streaks of wolf fur and were met in midway by their parents. The ecstatic dance of four wolves, beside themselves at the joy of reuniting in play and greeting, was something to see.

Beside me, Evie said, "This is magical."

"Indeed, it is."

I felt a twinge of regret that she wouldn't remember this experience. It seemed to me that, if anyone should get to retain the memory of a walk on December's snowy moors with magical wolves, it should be a person deeply affected.

"You seem like such a dog person," she said as we walked. "But I never knew that. Whenever I asked about getting a dog, you always said we couldn't."

"Because your father was quite adamant about being a canine-free household."

"Wow. I thought it was *you*."

I chuckled and shook my head. "No. I love dogs."

"I can see that now. You seem really happy, Mom. Like you belong here."

I breathed deeply through my nostrils and relished the sting of cold air. "I do belong here, Evie. Nothing has ever been more right unless it would be getting to share it with you."

"Aw. Have I told you I love it when you're sappy?"

I was laughing when we caught up to Lochlan. "Good morning, clerk!"

"Good morning, Magistrate!" He nodded at Evie and treated her to a disarming elven smile. To me he said, "You're doing a fine job with the pups. The parents are very proud."

"How do you know?" Evie asked.

It was a rookie question.

Lochlan tossed me an amused smile before telling her that, "Perhaps it's my imagination, but I indulge myself in the belief that they're understood."

Frey sat at her feet and looked up, signaling a demand for attention. Evie reached down and stroked the silky fur between her ears. Not to be excluded, Fen trotted right over and tried to nudge his nose between Evie's hand and Frey's head.

"You're a funny fellow, aren't you?" Evie was saying just as she was reaching to pet both wolves at the same time.

I turned to Lochlan. "The docket's ready to go?"

"Indeed, it is. It promises to be a very interesting week."

"In your experience, has there ever been a court meet that was not interesting."

He smiled. "I can't say I remember that."

"Just what I thought. What's the plan to sneak Evie inside?"

"All arranged. I've requested a week-long guest pass from Enya," he said.

"The singer?" Evie asked.

"No," Lochlan said, "the queen of Scotia fae. During the Hallowstide Court Meet, she bonded with your mother, albeit loosely because anything else would be frowned upon. This is now the second time the magistrate has tapped her for a favor."

"But who's counting?" I said sarcastically.

"You'd better be," Lochlan warned. "I assure you she is."

"I didn't ask her for this favor, Lochlan. You did."

"It was in your name. Same thing."

"No. It's not. If you're going to play free and loose with my ration of favors, you should at least ask."

"Noted."

"That's not ascent."

He smiled.

Evie laughed. "The two of you behave as if you've known each other forever."

I nodded. "I suppose it does feel like I've known Lochlan longer than I have. Perhaps because we're in the trenches together during court week."

"It's that contentious?" she asked. "That you use war metaphors to describe it?"

"Well..."

"There are tense moments," Lochlan said. "Especially since your mother is a bit of a loose cannon."

Evie barked out a laugh. "My mother is a bit of a loose cannon?" She sounded incredulous. "Are you sure we're talking about the same person?"

"I am not a loose cannon," I said in my defense.

Lochlan just smiled at Evie. "Come tomorrow and judge for yourself. It can be entertaining. Your mum is setting the fae world on its ear."

Evie looked at me like she'd never seen me before. The made sense. She had never seen the grand authority side of me. I might never have known it was a latent quality without the strange turn of events that had landed me here. I smiled to myself as I silently added the mantra, the Powers That Be are never wrong. I was coming to believe that was true.

CHAPTER SEVEN

Jewelry Junkies

AFTER LEAVING THE dogs at home and grabbing my backpack, we walked the short distance to village center.

"They go all out for seasonal occasions," I told her. "You should have seen it in October."

"It's like the best of all worlds. Picturesque and pedestrian, but with reliable power and good water delivery."

"And internet," I added. "Let's go to my shop first."

"Okay."

We went straight across the green and into the Hallows.

"Maggie!" I called.

As usual, she appeared in seconds. "Oh, aye. Here I am. And look who ye have with ye."

"Good morning," Evie said politely.

"Mornin', beautiful girl. Come for the proprietor's tour?"

"I suppose?" Evie checked with me.

"We sell two distinct categories of antiques and curious goods," I said, as I unwound my scarf. "Let's get out of these things before we overheat."

After removing our outerwear, I said, "Evie. It's so lucky that you and I are the same shoe size." I pulled the red shoes from my backpack. "When I first arrived I didn't yet have the ability to see magic kind in its true form. These shoes were an aid. If you want to borrow them, you'll be able to see things as human and as magic kind.

"We have items here in the shop that only magic kind can see. When humans come into the shop, it's as if those things don't exist. They're… invisible, I guess."

Evie had taken the shoes, sat down on a sturdy carved trunk, and was changing while I was talking. She'd just gotten both shoes on when Dolan stepped in to say something unusual had arrived in the morning's shipment. When she looked up at Dolan, she did a surprised double take, no doubt because of his goat slit irises. Seeing that surprise, his eyes immediately drifted down to the shoes.

"Really?" I asked. "Show me."

The four of us crowded into the work room.

"Perhaps 'tis no' ideal timin'," Maggie said as she glanced pointedly at Evie. "Do ye recall our recent talk about pieces arrivin' with notes attached?"

My eyes jerked to the chair sitting on the worktable. It was a balloon chair, old but almost cartoonish in shape. At some point it had been recovered because the wool tartan fabric looked new.

"Is that Clan Dunne?" I asked.

Dolan's eyes widened a little. "It is."

To get her up to speed as quickly as possible, I turned to Evie and gave her the Cliff's Notes version of how the shop inventory was magically replenished, and recounted my queries about the advisability of assuming new pieces were benign in nature.

"What did the note say?" I looked between Maggie and Dolan.

"That 'tis a lucky person who sits in the chair," Maggie replied.

I laughed out loud. "That is priceless. You've implied in previous conversations that notes only accompany pieces as a warning."

Maggie nodded thoughtfully, attention wandering back to the chair. "Has been the case. Until now."

"Okay. Before I tell you what I think, I want to hear your thoughts, Dolan."

Dolan had been standing with arms crossed, right hand absently stroking his goatee as he looked at the chair. Only his eyes moved as his gaze met mine.

"It's not just a chair."

I rolled my eyes, shifted my weight to one hip, and rested a hand there in a mime of, "Duh."

He shrugged. "At its core it's neither good nor bad, but it's unstable in terms of predictability. One person's idea of luck could be another person' idea of…"

"Doom?" Maggie asked, her tone sounding uncomfortably hopeful.

We all looked at her. No one answered.

"Your assessment isn't surprising, Dolan. Ambiguity is inferred by the devious nature of the note. As for me? I wouldn't sit in that chair if it promised me youth and immortality."

Evie turned to me, "You wouldn't?" I gaped at that reaction and was about to deliver a parental top-off lecture starting with something like, if that was her idea of good judgment… Then she smiled. "Just kidding."

My kid had a good, if odd, sense of humor.

Dragging my attention back to Dolan and Maggie, I said, "Was there any indication that this piece came from a different source than usual?" Maggie looked at Dolan who shook his head. "Was it crated with other things or by itself?"

"It was crated by itself, but in the exact same materials as other things in this delivery."

I nodded.

"What shall we do with it then? Maggie asked.

"What did you do with potentially harmful items in times past?"

"Threw them in the river," she said.

I laughed. "Evie's sense of humor is contagious." Maggie and Dolan didn't look amused. I sobered instantly. "You didn't!"

Maggie looked at Dolan as if wondering if she should

be sheepish, even though she wasn't. "We did," she said, cautiously.

"And you don't think there's such a thing as magical pollution?" I asked.

Maggie looked at Dolan then back at me. "Ne'er heard of such a thing."

"Then why didn't we throw the hobknobbit in the river?"

"Hobknobbit?" Evie asked.

"Ask me at lunch and I'll tell you about it," I said.

"Because the hobknobbit's energy wasn't ambiguous. It was bad," Dolan said.

"So, you determined that extraordinary precautions were advisable."

"Just so," Maggie said.

"Alright. That makes sense. But I'm still concerned about throwing items with question marks into the waterways. Aren't you concerned that effects might ripple outward? Maybe affecting humans and magic kind alike?" They both shook their heads. "I'll bite. Why not?"

"Water tends to neutralize magic," Maggie said matter-of-factly.

I looked at Evie, who shrugged. Apparently she didn't know that either.

"Oh," I said. "Well, in that case, throw it in the river?"

"Shame though," Maggie said. "Cute piece. Would've fetched a bright penny."

I nodded. "I like the tartan, too."

"Well, some of my liquid-lovin' cousins may sit in it from time to time." She laughed. "Perhaps they'll pretend to hold court."

In my head I began a countdown. Five, four, three...

"Your cousins?" Evie asked.

Whoomp. There it is.

"Oh. Well, you see..."

As Maggie began explaining her family tree to Evie, I moved closer to Dolan and asked, "Did we get anything else of note?"

"Mostly mundie. Got this though." He picked up an ordinary-looking brass knocker.

It was old, in need of a good polish, but had symbols on the plaque area where a surname would normally be found.

"What are these symbols?"

With his typical shrug, he said, "Mostly alchemical. For good luck."

"Real good luck. The kind anybody would like to have."

He gave me a small smile. "Yes."

"Do you want it?"

I caught him by such surprise he almost jerked. "Ah. Me?"

"Yes. You're making a home at the mill. Every house needs good luck."

He ran his calloused fingers over the door knocker and said, "Right. How'd you know?"

"That it's sort of like yours?" That was a good question. "Maybe Esme's intuition lessons are paying off?"

"I can pay for it."

"You could if I accepted payment. Consider it a bonus." I leaned in. "You know it's not against the rules for the magistrate to give gifts. Just the other way around."

"Well. I like it."

I imagined that was thank you in Dolan speak.

"You're welcome."

"Mom," Evie said, "Maggie's going to give me a turn

around the shop while I'm wearing the shoes."

"Sure. Go ahead."

While Evie was engaged with the Hallows' wares, magical and mundane, I was looking around the work-room asking questions about various pieces in different stages of repair.

Evie came up behind me. "I'm torn."

"About what?"

"I want to continue with the V.I.P tour of Hallow Hill, but I don't want to take the shoes off. I also don't want to try to walk in the snow in the shoes."

"Life is full of choices."

She cocked her head. "Are you ever gonna stop teach-ing?"

I studied her for a minute. "Is it time?"

"If you wanna be friends."

I thought about how the culture is wallpapered with let-that-go-it's-my-mother jokes and decided on the spot I didn't want to be avoided. Ever.

"Yes, I do. I will try to curtail the teaching, as you call it. If I slip, you have permission to remind me that friends don't do lectures or proverbs in excess."

"The good ones don't do those things at all. I mean unless you're about to do something like get married in Las Vegas while stoned."

"You know, after that sentence, every instinct in me is telling me you need me to carry on as your mother. Friendship is overrated."

"You *know* I would never do that. Right?"

"I *think* you would never do that, but you're the one who sowed doubt. Just now."

"Let's go back three minutes?"

I thought it over. "Deal."

"Friends?"

"Totally."

She giggled. "I'm doing the grownup thing and changing into sensible shoes."

"Good choice."

"But bring the others."

WE WENT ACROSS the street to The Braid. Evie regarded Braden's silver masterpieces reverently. I noticed she kept returning to a particular item. A chunky hammered medallion on a heavy silver necklace.

When it was time to go, I stopped in front of the necklace. "See anything you like here?"

She looked at me like she wasn't sure if it was a prelude to a gift or a cruel tease. "Uh…"

"I have something similar that was made by Braden's uncle. A little bigger maybe. I treasure it as much as anything I own. I wear it to court like a…"

While I was still searching for the word, Evie said, "Talisman."

"Right! Exactly!"

Braden arrived on the other side of the counter. Perfect timing. "It's my version of the goddess Danu's symbol. A triquetra with amber in the center. The silver has just enough copper added to give a blush of color that compliments the richness of the amber." She nodded, mesmerized. "Or the other way around. Needless to say, it's one of a kind."

She couldn't take her eyes off it. And I could see how the slight coppery color would be perfectly paired with the color of her hair.

I said, "Evie, if you love it the way I love my necklace, I want you to have it."

Her eyes got big. "I love it *so* much more than you love yours!"

Braden began taking the necklace down from its display. "You know what to do," I said, meaning send the bill to Maggie.

He nodded, then handed it to Evie. "Comes with the goddess's own personal blessing."

I chuckled at Braden. "Save it, Braden. We're not mundies."

Evie draped the necklace over her head and ran for the three-quarter mirror at the other end of the display. The artistry fired to life once it rested on top of Evie's charcoal grey sweater, the distressed background of the medallion, the uneven planes, grooves, and gouges, was picking up different light and changed with the slightest movement, even slow breathing.

"Thank you," Evie said, and I could tell she really meant it.

On the sidewalk, a blast of Arctic air temporarily stole my breath. I heard Evie gasp.

"Don't worry," I said. "It's usually over quickly. It just means Fie is in a snit about something or other."

"Fie? Oh, right. He's an air elemental."

I chuckled. "You remembered that's his preference. Everyone here really does call him wind devil."

The wind died away as quickly as it had risen. The town needed to put Olivia on retainer for the purpose of keeping Fie's temper balanced. Although I'm sure she wouldn't agree. It seemed to me that she enjoyed winding him up.

I stopped in front of Thomasin Cobb's shop and pointed to the door. "Never go in here," I said.

She leaned out so that she could see around me. "Why? What in there?"

"The nastiest little goblin anywhere. I'm told he makes the best boots in the world, but you have to pay a price far beyond coin to get them."

She grinned and started toward the door. "I want to see."

That was my Evie, headstrong to a fault.

I stepped in front of her, "No. Really. He. Will. Ruin. Your. Day."

"Come on," she insisted.

"Evie, remember the Soup Nazi?"

I knew she had because, growing up, she'd watched every episode of Seinfeld with me at least three times.

Her head jerked toward the door in delight. "Oh, my god. Are you serious?"

"Entirely. Unlike the people you met at the party, that little weirdo is not a friend. And he doesn't know who you are!"

"You mean that I'm connected?" she said under her breath like a mobster. Then laughed. "All the better. A real-life goblin Soup Nazi? Mom, I *can't* miss this. Wait here. I'll be right back."

I knew the folly of trying to get in the way of something Evie was set on doing. I'd been her mom for decades. So. I did as I was told and waited.

A full ten minutes later she arrived back on the side-walk, but unlike what I'd expected, which was to see her rattled and near tears, she took one look at me and began laughing so hard so couldn't breathe. She grabbed for her sides and waved at the air.

Eventually, when her breath settled, she said, "You should've come in. I should never have left you out here. I've never had so much fun!"

"Fun?" I looked back at the cobbler shop to be sure she'd entered the right door.

"Yeah." She still sounded excited. "By the end of our exchange he'd turned purple in the face and was so beside himself that he was kind of dancing around like this." I was treated to a sidewalk performance of the reenactment. If it was anything close to true, it was funny I had to admit. "Like the story about Rumpelstiltskin? I'll bet you anything they're related."

"Evie." She ran her arm through the crook of my elbow and snuggled close to keep us both warmer. "Poking at magic kind is a very, very bad idea. Some may seem comical, like him, but they're powerful. They could do things to you that couldn't be undone."

"Well, I guess I was lucky to get out in one piece."

"You're making light of it, but I agree. If you provoked him as hard as you say, it probably is lucky that you weren't scathed. At least as far as I can tell. Who knows what he's capable of? Now here's somebody worth seeing."

I opened the door to the florist. "Hello, Magistrate! Good morning, Evie."

"Hi," said Evie. "Wow. It looks and smells like paradise in here."

Lily chuckled. "Thank you."

I noticed she was in the process of making a wreath on the table behind the counter. "Hey. That wreath you're making looks just like the one…"

"Flibberdy-dijit," Lily said. I had to assume it was her version of cursing.

"What's wrong?"

"It's supposed to be a secret."

"What?" I asked. "The wreath? Why?"

"If I tell you, you have to swear that you will forget what I say." Since we both knew that was impossible and a silly exercise, but I agreed. "Keir saw how much you liked the one I made for John David and asked me to make one just like it for you."

"Awww," Evie said and turned to me for my reaction. "He's a keeper. Isn't he?"

I grinned. "We'll see." To Lily, I said, "Don't worry. The secret is safe. I played Rebecca in high school." Evie snorted and I gave her a look that said I didn't appreciate her lack of faith in my acting ability. "And it's every bit as pretty as the one we took to the manor last night."

Lily smiled brightly. "It was a fun party." She looked at Evie. "Wasn't it?"

"The best," Evie said. "And some time I would love it if you would show me your pixie form. It would be a big thrill."

"I don't see how I can say no to that. I haven't fed the plants pixie dust in two days. So you can watch if you like."

Setting down the florist shears she'd been holding, Lily went straight to the door where she turned the sign around and locked the latch. Faster than human eyes could track she'd turned into her pixie form and was flitting about leaving pixie dust on the potted plants.

"Mom," Evie breathed with that reverence she reserved for impossible things. "Are you the luckiest person alive?"

As I watched Lily, I smiled and said, "I think so."

Lily flew a few spirals then hovered in front of me. I held out my palm as Lochlan had taught me to do. When she landed, I said, "Now I know your secret for the happiest plants anywhere. Magic."

The pixie giggled.

To Evie I said, "I know a lot was going on last night and I don't know how much info you processed, but Lily and Ivy, Lochlan's wife, are sisters. You should see the garden across from my house in warm weather. It's indescribable."

"Well, I will see it in warm weather. Right?"

"Oh," I said. "Of course!"

It wasn't a lie. If she decided to definitely continue school in England, she would see Ivy's garden in full bloom. She just wouldn't know that magic was involved.

Lily flew back to the front door, changed to the larger, wingless, version of herself, unlocked the door and turned the sign to OPEN.

Walking toward the front, I said, "We're famished and on the way for winter soup at Molly's. Want to join us?"

"Thank you, Magistrate." With a knowing smile, she said, "I'm busy with a wreath today, but I'm on the schedule for lunch the Monday after court week."

"Schedule?" Evie looked at me.

"She doesn't know about Legendary Lunch?"

I chuckled every time somebody called it that. "Not yet. I'm going to tell her all about it over lunch at the pub.

See you later."

"Shhhh," she said.

I mimed zipping my lips as I held the door open for Evie.

Molly smiled and said, "Magistrate!" as we rushed in out of a fresh gust of wind. Sure enough, Fie was sitting at the bar looking like he was in a snit.

I waved.

She pointed toward my favorite table by the fire, that was unoccupied. I grinned, nodded, and guided Evie over, explaining all the reasons why it was my favorite table.

"I can see that," she said as she sat.

Within seconds Jeff was at table's edge.

Evie looked up. "Hey. It's the Lorcan who pranked my mom."

He smiled. "That would be me."

"Evie," I admonished. "Keep your voice down. Occasionally the pub gets humans who are either tourists or passing through. You need to take inventory and make sure you can account for everyone before you say such things loud enough to be heard."

"Sorry," she said. "But I don't see how that would hurt

anything. Since nobody ever heard of Lorcans."

"I've heard of Lorcans," Jeff said, and it was impossible to tell if he was being facetious. I thought to myself that perhaps he'd shifted into a humorless waiter. "What would you like?" he said.

"To see the menu?" she asked.

He dashed off but was back before we could get involved in a new conversation.

The impressive list of lunch menu offerings was one big page. Lighter fare on front. Stick-to-the-ribs heartier meals on the back.

"This looks yummy," she said.

"Jeff?" He turned toward my voice. "What do you have for dessert?"

"Boysenberry cobbler with vanilla ice cream we made ourselves. A bit ago."

"I'll have that right after a cup of winter soup."

He nodded and looked at Evie.

"What's good?" she asked.

"I've been eating here long enough to say this honestly. Everything. Keir is doing his take on stir fry tonight. It's heavy. Don't expect Asian. Do expect flour, fat, salt, meat, and thin slices of potato with a few English peas scattered on top. More for color than nutrition."

"Yeah. Thanks for the warning." To Jeff, she said. "I'll have salad."

"Which one?" I asked.

"The one with mixed greens, walnuts, purple cabbage, purple onion, and vinaigrette." To Jeff, she said, "And an extra spoon when you bring her dessert."

"Good and good." He finished as he was leaving.

Evie watched him go then turned back to me. "Have you ever wondered why somebody who could be anything, literally, would choose to be a waiter in a tiny village pub?"

"Actually, I have wondered that. Decided it was his business."

"I guess. So, what's this about Legendary Lunch?"

I told her all about Olivia, her cooking skills and how the lunches had come to be.

"First, it's kind of hard to imagine John David being stone faced and mute. He seems so..."

"Lively?"

She laughed. "Good one, Mom. Yeah. Lively. When I asked him how old he was, you know I was kidding around. I didn't know he's older than most of the stuff at the British museum."

"Well…"

"Does Molly not mind that you do these lunches?"

"I'd been concerned about that in the beginning, but she assures me it's fine with her. She's even come once or twice. Molly's one of my favorites. She gives me intuition lessons."

"I don't think I can tell when you're joking anymore."

I chuckled as Jeff set down drinks, a loaf of artisan bread with locally churned butter and left.

"I'm not joking. I think it's working. I mean sometimes I do have an inner guidance apparatus. I don't know its nature or how it works. But I do believe there's something there and she's helping me find it and amplify it."

"Cool."

"It is. We have people around who really do know stuff though. In fact I thought we'd stop off at Esmerelda's on the way home."

"The weaver? Who made my dress?"

"Yes. Special clothing is what her shop is about, but it's really only one of her gifts. When I have a problem and no sign of a solution, I run there first. I'd warn you about her dry personality and the fact that she has *no* sense of humor, but anybody who thinks an encounter with Thomasin Cobb is funny doesn't need a warning label about terse personalities."

"Thomasin Cobb," she repeated, shaking her head and laughing silently. "He's a kick."

"What's that?" Fie was pulling up a chair. "I'm not joining you for lunch. Just heading off and thought I'd say hello. Are you extending the proper cautions about the little bugger?"

"First," I said, "you've made giant leaps of assumption if you think my daughter is the sort to heed cautions. She does what she wants, including having a chat with the cobbler."

Fie's head jerked to Evie. "You talked to him?"

"Oh," I jumped in. "Far more. She provoked him to the point where he turned purple and started doing a bizarro little dance."

"Evie," Fie said. "I'm not sure that's entirely safe for you."

I chimed in with my agreement. "Exactly, or rather,

close to what I said."

"Okay." Evie lifted her hands. "I get it. Angry goblins can do ugly stuff."

With a nod, I said, "Everything okay with you, Fie?"

"Why do you ask?" he said.

"You know the answer to that. The wind almost knocked us over twice when we were out this morning."

He looked sheepish. "I'm sorry. Sometimes Olivia gives me... What was that you called it?"

"Mood swings?"

"Yes. That. So, my other reason for stopping by was to let you know that we've organized an Evie roster for the week." He smiled at both of us. "We have a clipboard and everything."

"And an Evie roster is?" I asked.

"One of us will be with her every minute to help her get around, answer questions, and you know..."

"Make sure she stays out of trouble?" I offered.

"Well. Yes." He looked at Evie. "I'm first up. So, you'll be spending the day with me tomorrow. I'll pick you up at half past nine. That will give us time to drive to Tregeagle and get situated before court convenes."

"That's very kind of you," Evie said. "I'll be ready."

"I'm grateful, Fie. To you and everybody on the clip-board."

As he stood to go, he said, "It's part of having the honor of living in the same town as the magistrate." He smiled. "And everybody wants to insure their place in Legendary Lunch rotation."

"I don't know why. You could have Olivia's cooking anytime," I said.

"There's more to Legendary Lunches than food, you know." I hadn't given it a lot of thought, but of course there was a desirable social aspect. With a nod to Evie, he said, "See you tomorrow."

"You've got real friends here," Evie said.

"Yeah."

"So, tomorrow?"

"Uh-huh?"

"What are you wearing?"

I laughed softly. She was my girl. "I'm wearing judge's robes. And the wolf medallion I told you about. You? No matter what you wear you'll feel right at home."

While I described the period costumes and outrageous

clothes she could expect to see, we ate soup and salad, respectively then shared a boysenberry cobbler. I was sure I'd be seeing that cobbler in my dreams.

"Remember, you're not going to be able to see what's going on without the red shoes on. Esme may have some suggestions for how you can wear them without your feet being cold."

IT SEEMED UNUSUAL to find Esme working at one of the looms, but there she was. No need to announce that we'd arrived.

"Hey."

She looked us both up and down and, after an awkward pause, said, "Hey," in the most underwhelming, uninspired way imaginable. She was not making a good impression. Not that she'd care.

"Evie is coming to court this week. In order to see and hear what's going on, she'll need to wear the red shoes." Esme resumed her weaving. "I was wondering if you have a good suggestion for how to wear the shoes and be warm at the same time."

She stopped. "Let me see them."

I pulled the shoes from the bag. She took one, looked it over, handed it back and said, "I'll send something over later."

"Oh. Well, thank you. That was more than I was expecting."

"Was it?" she asked."

"Yes." I was feeling a little defensive.

"You weren't expecting to have the girl's future told?"

"What? No!"

"Wait a minute," Evie said. "You can do that?"

"No. We didn't come for that. I just wanted Esme to see the shop and the clothes while I asked about something to keep her from taking a chill."

"What do you want?" Esme looked past me and was speaking directly to Evie.

I remembered the day Maggie had dragged me into the shop for the first time. Esmerelda had predicted I'd find love. I laughed at her and practically called her a charlatan, something she regularly reminds me of.

"The future's not set in stone, Evie," I said.

My daughter's attention had fixed on the spinning wheel in the back of the store. "Can I touch it?" She asked, motioning in that direction.

What happened to Esmerelda's face was the closest thing to a full out smile I'd ever seen. She nodded at Evie and slowly followed.

"You're drawn to it because it figures prominently in fairytales," Esme said. Evie nodded. "Spinning is a big part of the history or both humans and magic kind, but make no mistake. It's magical for both. For almost a thousand years an unmarried woman was known as a spinster because a woman without a husband spent her days at the wheel. Women understand spinning. Even noblewomen, who wanted for nothing, would spin. To the uninitiated, it might appear that we are simply spinning yarn, but more happens when we spin. Magic is awakened by creativity moving in circular motion and it comes to see what's being made. Sometimes it affixes itself to the yarn as its wound onto the spindle. That's one of the reasons why old spindles are so prized by witches. The residue of magic remains for a very long time."

I'd never heard Esmerelda speak so many words at once. The cadence of her voice was hypnotic, and I was as drawn in as Evie.

"The Norns are the three goddesses of fate, worshipped by the northern tribes, who spin the futures of individuals and worlds into reality. They've been called Moirai and Parcae by Greeks and Romans, Fates in modern times, but no matter the names by which they're called, outcomes, lifespans, futures are made manifest by the turning of the wheel."

Esme reached out and gave the wheel a spin. The movement of the wheel was captivating. A second before Evie reached toward the wheel, I realized the energy had changed in the room. It didn't feel heavy like a dream that can't be escaped, but it did feel heavier than it had before. And there was definitely a drowsy, dreamlike quality in the atmosphere. Feelings, colors, even thoughts, were not as sharp. I remembered the story about *Sleeping Beauty* and the prick she received when the witch was giving her a demonstration.

Just before Evie's hand touched the spindle, I said, "NO!"

I don't know what made me reach out and bat her hand away. Maybe instinct. Maybe irrational, superstitious fear. I felt embarrassed and exposed for having been so easily caught up in the spell Esme had been casting. Whether she'd intentionally released magic into her lecture was something I'd have to sort out later.

When the surprise of my outburst receded, all three of us laughed, even Esmerelda. The two of them probably guessed why I was afraid for Evie to touch the blasted contraption. Evie probably thought it was charming. Since she'd chosen to make a life's work of sorting out the impact of fairytales on our psyches, she was surely well-aware of the fears and shadows that lurk in the recessed corridors of our minds. Vigilant. Waiting for the right opportunity to make themselves known and make us look ridiculous in the process.

Regardless of Esme's tribute to the connection be-tween the spinning wheel and the feminine divine, I chose to believe it was a blasted contraption. Nothing more. I told myself that whatever altered state had been induced and encouraged by Esme, for a reason yet to be deter-mined, the spinning wheel was just an antique. Nothing more.

As my consciousness, and the feeling of being firmly grounded in this reality, returned fully, so did logic. That's when I realized how preposterous it was for me to be insistent that the spinning wheel was an assembly of wood and iron. Nothing more. As proprietor of a shop that sells antiques and curious goods, both mundane and magical, I should be the last person to mount a skeptic's apologetic.

I brought my attention fully back to the moment when part of my mind heard Evie saying, "Should I be wary about having my future told? I mean, not that you agreed to do it. Of course, I'm intrigued."

If Evie thought the hand snatch was interference, she'd be surprised at the lengths I'd go to when it came to making sure Esmerelda did not do a reading on Evie. Though I like to think of myself as a modern, intelligent woman, I do have beliefs that some would call superstitious. My aversion to fortune telling had to do with a suspicion that mystics sometimes plant thoughts that take root and manifest, not because the future was written, but because their 'vision' was believed to be destiny.

Esme looked at Evie with an affection I'd never seen her express. I wasn't sure if I should feel pride, gratitude, or wariness. It did force me to ask myself to what extent I trusted Esmerelda. It had been true for months that I'd run to her for counsel and problem-solving. But…

"You don't need me to tell your future, daughter of the magistrate. Your mother has the most reliable tool anywhere."

I do?

As if Esme heard my silent question, she turned to me and said, "The pink crystal."

The pink crystal? The one that was supposed to tell the future of virgins?

Evie turned to me. "You have a pink crystal that'll tell my future?"

"Um… Maybe we can talk about this in private. At home."

Seeing the slight scowl that had come to be familiar in just a short time, I knew there was no doubt my Evie was going to end up with pronounced WTF lines between her brows. Just. Like. Mine. And I hoped she was going to enjoy the next couple of decades of walking around looking like she'd been airbrushed.

She gave me a confused look, but silently agreed. To Esme, she said, "Your shop is beautiful. Your stories, too. Even if you're not going to read my future, I'd really love to have the opportunity to interview you before I go back to school.

Esmerelda cocked her head. "Back to school in New England? Or back to school in England."

Evie laughed. "You're a mind reader. Are you telepathic in the sense that you can send as well as receive?"

Esme smiled. "Yes. I will answer questions that I want to answer. Yes. I pick up stray thoughts. Sometimes. Yes. I can send thoughts if communicating with someone who shares similar abilities."

Evie chuckled. "What's it like to have a friend who knows what you're thinking, Mom?"

"Interesting," I said, hoping that Esme was reading the thought that I saw a serious talk in our future.

My phone rattled in my bag. I saw that it was Keir and stepped away, not really wanting to leave Evie alone with Esmerelda.

"Hey," I said.

"Salutations, Magistrate."

"Oh. We're doing formal."

"Just getting into my role. Tomorrow morning at court I'm not your extraordinarily handsome snuggle buddy. I'm enforcer to the supreme decider over all contested matters in the entirety of the magical world."

"Wow. Take a breath."

"I'm headed over to Tregeagle to doublecheck that we're all set for court week kickoff."

"I'm hearing sports terminology creep." He squinted and shook his head slightly. "If you aren't careful, it will take over. I've seen it happen," I deadpanned.

"Okay. Back for dinner. I told Evie you're making sephalian stir fry."

"If you want to talk creep, creepier, creepiest, you get the prize for saying sephalian stir fry."

My hand flew to my mouth. "You know I didn't mean it like *that*."

He wasn't about to let me off easy.

"Indeed." I loved the way his eyes twinkled when he teased. "I should be back and in the kitchen in plenty of time. If not, I'll text and pick something up from Molly. Or I could call Olivia."

"Let's don't bother Olivia on her day off. She's in the middle of a courtship, perhaps the first and only of her entire life."

"With luck, dinner won't be an issue. I'll be there in plenty of time to delight the palate and thrill the tummies."

"Big claims," I teased.

"I always deliver on my promises. As you well know."

I could not engage in intimate talk with Esme and Evie a few feet away. So I said, "Um, yeah. I know. Don't go to the carnival and forget the time."

He laughed and ended the call.

"All set?" I asked Evie, meaning, "Let's get out of here."

"Sure," she said agreeably. "Thanks for the yarn, Esmerelda."

I laughed both at Evie's most excellent pun and also at the confused look on Esme's face. As we reached the door, I told Evie under my breath so that Esme wouldn't hear, "Good one!"

Evie's use of pun to describe the experience we'd had with the spinning wheel left me hoping that she'd forget all about the pink crystal thing, or discount it as gypsy ramblings.

No such luck.

CHAPTER EIGHT

Jersey Devil Jinga Linga

W E HUNG UP our outerwear in the mudroom, exchanged Ugg slip-ons for snow boots, and went straight to the kitchen to warm up something hot, liquid, and delicious.

"Tea of coffee?" I asked.

"I'm thinking tea. If I'm going to finish school in England, I need to go native."

"You're still thinking Oxford?"

"Well, yeah. Did something happen to make you think I'd changed my mind?"

"Um, no. Nothing in particular. I just wasn't sure it was definite."

"Next week, after your magistrate duty is done, I thought we'd drive over to Oxford together and look around. I mentioned it. Don't you remember?"

"Um. Of course, I remember."

"Is there some reason you don't want to go? I thought it'd be a great outing. I mean, a lot of the buildings may be closed for Christmas. The campus will probably look deserted, but that might make it all the more fun. From a certain point of view."

"Very true. And you're right. It would be a fun day trip. So you're saying you won't make a final call until you've had a visit. Even if it's during student break."

"Yeah. That's what I'm saying. We'll have a good day and see how it goes."

"That is a plan."

"Right?"

"Right. Next week we'll pick a day to be scholarly tourists."

She chuckled. "Now about the pink crystal thing."

Saved by the locomotive whistle of my very fanciful tea kettle.

It took five minutes or so to gather the makings of a tea including a glass-dome-covered tray of Olivia's cookies. Fudge with dark chocolate chips, oatmeal with brandy-drenched raisins, and colorful Yule sugar cookies, all on a real white linen and lace doily. You've got to hand it to Olivia. She's got style that doesn't shrink from extra work.

That gave me five minutes to figure out how I was going to approach the subject of the crystal.

When I sat down and poured hot water into the Royal Doulton cup sitting in front of Evie, she said, "I'm sensing avoidance behavior."

"Avoidance behavior?" I dodged. "Who talks like that?"

"Somebody who recognizes it when I see it. And, in case you missed it, your response was confirmation."

"Hmmm. Well. It's problematic and complicated and has the potential to touch on sensitive subjects."

After a sip of tea, she said, "You know me well enough to know I'm not going to just let this go and forget about it."

Truer words were never spoken. I did know that about her. One of the reasons why she'd scored a coveted and rare seat at Oxford was because she had a rat terrier personality. Once she was bitten by the idea of wanting a thing, she wouldn't turn loose if it took her straight to hell. It was a personality trait with paired behaviors, like a two-sided coin. An asset when the goal was overachievement. A liability when reason would dictate that it was time to release something not working and move on.

"Alright. But don't blame me if the explanation ventures into awkward territory that may not be any of my business."

After staring for a few beats, she said, "Okaaaaay."

"If that means you'd like to withdraw the inquiry, that's okey dokey with me. We can talk about something else. Like which ones of my neighbors you want to talk to."

She was shaking her head. "There's no stopping now." I was afraid she'd say exactly that. "Tell me about the pink crystal." After a slight pause, she added, "Please."

"Have you ever heard of kelpies?"

I told her the entire story about the young Irish prince and his ill-fated scheme to be king of kelpies if he couldn't be king of Irish fae and ended with my visit from the Jersey Devil assassin and his gift. Correction, alleged assassin.

At this point in the story, I left the kitchen long

enough to retrieve the rock.

I set it on the table like it was part of the tea service.

Evie stared long and hard before saying, "It's… beauti-ful."

She turned and looked at the flames in the counter-height fireplace behind her and I knew she was comparing the look of the actual flames in the fireplace to their reflection off the crystalline planes of the J.D.'s gift.

When she turned back, she said, "Are you worried that there's a crazed kelpie gunning for you?"

I laughed. If I had been worried, the wording of her question struck me as so funny that I forgot all about it.

"Not really. First, if you'd met the monster in person, you'd understand why I feel fairly confident in his special-ized abilities. Second, I have a lot of security around. There's Keir. It doesn't get more formidable than that."

"Keir's not always here."

"That's true, but I have two dogs."

"They're puppies. You said so yourself."

"They're not fully mature, but as you well know, when they're in wolf form they're already bigger than you'd expect a full grown wolf to be. But the biggest security feature is the house itself. It wouldn't let anybody in who wasn't welcomed by me."

"I have a solution to keep you safe no matter what."

"No matter what?" My question had the sound of a child's eagerness. The question of Keaira laying in wait was always at the back of my mind and it was a disquietude I'd love to shed.

"Simple. Stay away from water."

"A good idea. But I've seen kelpies run across land. Granted it was a short distance, but still."

"Well, until we think of something airtight, stay *far* away from water."

"Will do." I smiled. "So. Now that that's settled. How do you feel about naps?"

The room had grown darker and I knew what that meant. Every afternoon the clouds thickened before the daily snowfall that gave Hallow Hill a fresh layer of pristine white.

She narrowed her eyes. "You didn't really think I'd be put off the scent that easily."

"Hoped you might be."

"That would be a rookie mistake."

"Have you been picking up sports talk from Keir?"

"Not per se. If you talk to males post potty training, unless they're highly unusual like Dad, you're going to pick up sports lingo. It's a good resource, full of drama, great analogies, and metaphors ripe and ready for easy picking."

"No argument."

"So. The awkward thing you mentioned that might not be any of your business?" I nodded. "The answer is yes. I'm a candidate for using the pink crystal to tell my fortune." I'd been so sure that the answer was no. "I can tell by your expression you're surprised."

I saw no reason not to be honest. "I guess I am."

"Well, I'm not ashamed of being a virgin."

"Oh, no, gods, that's not... Of course, you have no reason to be ashamed." I twisted my body in the chair to face her more fully. "There's been a mere passage of two generations since there was real shame in being an unmarried woman who was *not* being a virgin. You're living in a time when you get to choose without fear of judgement. I just thought... Because I knew you had boyfriends."

"Boyfriends who come and go. Frequently."

"Well, I just assumed you were shopping around."

"No. Every time I refused to take that step, the boy I was with fumed, made a big fuss, called me names, then moved on."

"I see why you call them jerks." My eyes flew up to meet hers. "Are you afraid?"

She smiled. "Not in the way you think. My fear is making the wrong decision and having regrets. Every time I say no and the guy acts like a toddler who didn't get his way, I'm relieved he wasn't the one. You know, you listen to other girls talk. They say things like, 'He turned out to be such a lying, cheating, loose-lipped loser and I really wish I hadn't given it up for him'." You hear that often enough and you start to think that maybe you want to know *who* you're screwing *before* you do it."

"Evie. I thought you were just a college kid. But you're a lot more. Seems like, when I wasn't looking, you grew up."

"So, you don't think I'm weird?"

"Far from it."

"Well, now that that's settled. How do you turn the

crystal on?"

"You want to see your future?"

"Well, yeah."

"And you can't be dissuaded?"

"No."

"Well," as Dolan would say, "it didn't come with an instruction manual."

"You don't know how to turn it on?"

"Nope."

"Then what's it good for?"

"Beats me. Let's have naps." I started to get up, hoping to call the matter closed.

"Hold on. How about if I try just asking it out loud? To read my future?"

That sounded way too simple to work. So, naturally, I was all for it.

"Sure. Give that a try."

She picked up the crystal, said, "Heavy," and set it down directly in front of her. "Tell me my future."

For an instant I thought I saw a flare in the fireplace over her right shoulder, but just as quickly discounted it as imagination.

The doorbell sang out.

I grinned at Evie. "That'll be Lily with my wreath."

When I reached the front door, the snow was falling, as predicted, in big fluffy flakes suitable for a Currier and Ives holiday.

I opened the door wide with a big grin on my face, which immediately fell away.

"Afternoon, Magistrate," said Diarmuid.

My dogs rushed past me to greet Diarmuid on the porch like the celebrity that he was.

"Ah, Diarmuid. Hi. I, um, wasn't expecting you."

"Oh. I know. I will no' be stayin'. Just stoppin' by to let you know my cousin is settlin' in with Ilmr's bunch and all is well."

"It's very nice of you to keep me posted." That was supposed to be a hint that I was occupied. I was about to say, "Thank you for coming," when I realized he was leaning to my right, looking at something over my right shoulder with interest.

Oh. Hell to the no!

I had a good idea what he was looking at, but a quick look back confirmed that, yep, the fae world's biggest player was taking a bead on my daughter.

"Diarmuid…"

"Are ye no' goin' to invite me in then?"

Even somebody as politically inexperienced as I am would grasp how unwise it would be to turn the king of Irish fae away.

"Of course. You know you're always welcome." He smiled and stepped in, without ever taking his eyes off Evie. When I closed the door, I said, "Diarmuid, this is my daughter, Evie."

"Evangeline," she corrected, looking at him like she was Rapunzel having just touched ground, seeing a handsome, young male for the first time.

My impulse to repeat that in question form was stopped just before the guest cottage would've disappeared. That would be hard to explain.

Without looking directly at me, Diarmuid said, "She's, em…"

"Human. That's right. Can I get you tea?"

He looked at me then looked at Evie who nodded. I could have throttled her.

He was evidently pleased by her encouraging gesture

because he smiled and said, "I would love a black tea with clotted cream and a sprig of mint."

Geez. Royals.

"I'm pretty sure I have black tea. I might have some kind of fresh mint. I don't know. Clotted cream? Definitely not."

Without looking away from Evie, he said, "I'll be happy with whate'er you have." He began unwinding his beautiful tartan scarf, like he planned to stay for a while.

I lit the living room fire before leaving the room. "Please sit," I told him. "Evie, Diarmuid has just ascended to the throne of the Irish fae. He's king. And leader of the Wild Hunt."

I could see by the way Diarmuid pulled himself up that he wanted Evie to be impressed by that. I glanced her way to see if she was starstruck.

Her eyes had widened. "You're the… Di Anu?" She was, starstruck that is.

Diarmuid looked first shocked then pleased. "If you're human, how would you know this, Evangeline?"

"I've studied the history of your, um, kind. In depth," she added.

"Wouldn't you two like to sit down?" I prompted again.

Evie sat at the end of one of my two facing sofas. Diarmuid sat in the big chair closest to her. My dogs got as close to him as was physically possible without sitting on his feet. Were they gazing at him adoringly?

As I left the room, I could hear the beginning of semi-normal conversation.

"So. You know my mother?"

"No' as well as I thought. I did no' know she has a beautiful daughter. One who's also an authority on fae."

"Oh. I wouldn't say I'm an authority. I suspect there's a lot that's unknown. To, um, us. But I'd like to be."

I went straight for my phone, shut myself in the larder off the kitchen, and called Keir.

"Hello?"

"Keir. You're not going to believe this. Diarmuid came for another visit."

"Oh?"

"And, although you were way off base being afraid he was interested in me, we do have a huge freaking problem. Because he's interested in Evie and I'm freaking out."

"Alright." He sounded calm. That was a good sign. "Let him have his flirtation. His interest in feminine company never lasts for longer than five minutes."

"Five minutes?"

"That was meant as illustrative. Not literal. It's not as big a problem as you might think. Let him feel admired by Evie. He'll have his tea, go about his business, and forget all about it."

"Really?"

"Yes."

"Okay. You're sure?"

"He hasn't varied his pattern for nigh to a millennium."

"That does sound like he's set in his ways. And how could somebody that experienced possibly be interested in a twenty-two-year-old?"

"Precisely. No worries."

I felt buoyed by that reassurance. After all, Keir would know. I got the king's tea together on a tray and carried it to the living room. He and Evie were laughing about something as I entered.

"Here we are," I said brightly. "Black tea, a spring of

spearmint, and coffee creamer. No clotted cream. Sorry."

"Please do no' apologize. I should no' have assumed."

Wow. Manners from one of the royal fae? What could possibly be next?

As I sat on the sofa opposite Evie, Diarmuid turned his attention back to her. "Will ye be attendin' the court meet then?"

"Yes. Looking forward to it."

"Tomorrow?" he pressed.

I searched my memory of what was on the docket for the next day. "So far as I know, there are no cases involving the House of Bayune scheduled to be heard tomorrow."

"'Tis true, the gravity of my responsibility is serious and I think 'tis best to stay apprised."

"A wise approach," I agreed, with little other choice.

"You're welcome to sit the gallery dedicated to my house. 'Tis very close to the magistrate's bench and has an admirable view."

"It's so kind and generous of you to make that offer, Diarmiud, but our unelected mayor, Fie Mistral, is going to escort her to the proceedings tomorrow."

He nodded. "Very well. Tuesday."

"I'm afraid the Hallow Hill residents have spoken for every day this week. They're very fond of her." I smiled.

I had the sense that Diarmuid was becoming irritated, but his smile didn't falter. "Aye. I can understand why." He looked at Evie. "Perhaps Saturday, after court meet is concluded, we could…"

Before I could interrupt with an excellent reason why that would be completely and utterly impossible for all eternity, Evie was nodding and saying, "Yes. I'm free Saturday."

Diarmuid grinned like he'd won a prize. "'Tis my lucky day then. What would ye like to do? Name any-thin'."

"Something magical."

He chuckled. "Come now, beautiful lass. Give me somethin' hard so I can prove myself."

So, he can prove himself? What the…?

Her responding giggle told me she was buying what he was selling.

That's when it hit me like a bucket of cold water had just been emptied over my head.

Evie asked to know her future. The doorbell rang within seconds and there stood Diarmuid. I tried to tell myself that was the coincidence of all coincidences, but the Jersey Devil didn't impress me as the sort to drop off gifts that either prank or misfire.

I certainly wasn't ready to believe that the 'Di Anu' was my Evie's future. So, I decided to make a list of reasons why I might accept that such an outlandish turn of events was possible. Number one was the hard-to-ignore timing of Diarmuid's arrival. Number two was the sober, if rough around the edges, authenticity of the gift giver.

These two things could be explained away. I made a deal with myself that, if a third reason reared its head, I'd have to consider the possibility.

Damn.

WHEN DIARMUID LEFT, I sat down and stared at Evie.

"What?" she said feigning innocence in a way that was believable to be disturbing.

"He's not a cute guy you ran into in the ancient books section at one of the Oxford colleges' libraries."

"I know." She sounded a little indignant that I thought

perhaps she didn't know that. "He's Joel Kinnaman! Only better. And I can't believe I said that."

"He is in fact the most powerful fae in their world. *Almost* a god."

"Yeah. I know that, too."

"Then what are you doing?" She said nothing. "Tell me something. This is right up your alley. What *always* happens when male gods get involved with human girls?"

"I take your point. But first, there are exceptions."

"Like what?"

"Eros and Psyche. And second, I haven't agreed to anything but coffee."

I barked out a laugh. "I didn't hear anything about coffee," I scoffed. "Show me magic," I mimicked her. "That's easy. Give me something hard," I mimicked him.

She laughed.

"This is not funny. He's the LEADER OF THE WILD HUNT for cripes sake! He doesn't do COFFEE!"

"We'll see."

"Evie, you don't know anything about him. He has a reputation in the fae world for being the world's biggest player. His stock and trade is dalliance."

She rolled her eyes. "I know who he is, Mom. The leader of the Wild Hunt is like… the ultimate bad boy."

"That's right. Which means this is foolhardy even for you."

"Should I resent that?"

"No. You should admit that you have a history of leaping before you look."

"Really? And that's why I'm the only person I know who's my age and a virgin?"

Oh, man. She had a point. A really, really, really good point.

"Alright. You do have your moments when you're wise beyond your years as well."

"That's right!"

"But Evie. You're a human girl. From their perspective, that means powerless. In what universe do you think it would be a good idea for a powerless young woman to have coffee with an all-powerful fae king?"

"When you put it that way, it sounds crazy. And if it was somebody else, I'd tell them not to be an idiot. But I have to go with my intuition on this one, Mom. It doesn't *feel* crazy. And it's not like I'm going to let him punch my

V card." She began examining her nails. "Unless he gives an oath of undying love with a built-in punishment of automatic agony if he ever cheats on me."

I felt my mouth fall into a gape.

She looked at me through her lashes with a sly smile. "Gotcha."

I was going to have to do something about being everybody's favorite target for pranking. Either I was giving off gullible vibes or I was *actually* gullible, which would be worse, of course. I was thus engaged in serious self-reflection when I heard the back door open. I sat calmly and waited for Keir knowing he'd find us like a homing beacon.

When he came in, he waved and went to stand with his back to the fire.

"How'd you find things?" I asked.

"Everything's in good order. Ready for tomorrow. The carnival is pretty. The belly dancers have goosebumps." He was joking, of course. Magic kind don't get goosebumps. "How'd things go here?"

"Depends on your point of view," I said offhandedly as if my day had presented nothing at all unusual. "Evie, who all of a sudden wants to be known by her birth name, said yes to a date with Diarmuid."

Keir looked at Evie. "You didn't."

"Tell him to call me Evangeline? I did," she said defiantly.

"No," Keir said with mock patience. "I mean that you didn't seriously agree to a date with that bloody blaggard and you know that's what I mean."

"Not you, too," she said. "I'm not a teenager. And I'm not telling either one of you who to have coffee with." She huffed and looked between us as if she was in charge of the reproach. "I'm getting the message you don't like him. Consider it noted and I will keep that in mind. While deciding for myself."

This was making me wonder if, in Evie's mind, coffee was used as a substitute for other kinds of activities which men and women share.

"Well, that is so," he said. "There's simply the fact that you're human and he's…"

"I really don't think the two of you have checked in with your own reality. My mother is human, Enforcer." Evie said. "You keep saying that Diarmuid is all-powerful, but that's not really true. Let's play a game. In a head-to-head smackdown who'd win? The Di Anu or the sephalian?"

I looked at Keir, who simply blinked. He couldn't deny it. He only used his awesome power to make sure the magistrate's rulings were enforced, as indicated by the title, but still. Head-to-head smackdown? Might as well declare him the winner now because there's no contest.

I wasn't going to be able to stop her. It seemed I'd role modeled this behavior. As I thought back, I realized that Keir and I began with lunches and coffees.

My hopes were pinned on a number three not showing up on my list of reasons to consider Diarmuid being Evie's future.

Lily did come around with the wreath and I did a masterful job of pretending I knew nothing about it. I should have been nominated for an award.

Esmerelda pressed Braden into service to deliver a solution to red shoes, as promised. I rewarded him with a bag of Olivia's cookies, and you would've thought it was an American Express gift card valued at a thousand pounds.

Esme had sent winter white cashmere to-the-knee leg warmer/shoe covers with lace trim. They were designed so that they fitted over the shoes, when on, and had an ingenious elastic strap that looped under the arch to hold them in place.

"These are beautiful," Esme put them to her cheek. "And soooooo soft. But they'll be filthy before I even leave the house."

I picked up the handwritten card and read out loud. "Don't worry about dirt or stains. They come with a repellent." I looked up. "See? No problem. She's a genius."

"You mean they've got like magic Scotch Guard? Is that even possible?"

I laughed at her. "Okay. So you have no trouble with Lorcans, vampires, brounies, pixies, wind devils, sephalian, and the *Wild Hunt*? But you draw the line at magic socks?"

She laughed with me. "This lifestyle of yours takes some getting used to."

We had Keir's very fattening but very satisfying sephalian stir fry, watched *Trapped in Paradise*, and went to bed. I told Evie that we'd be leaving ahead of her and to not worry about locking the house. It would take care of itself.

In bed, Keir said, "You're still awake, aren't you?"

"Yeah."

"Worried about the Diarmuid date thing, I suppose."

"How could I not?"

"Look at it this way. Of all the things the new king might do, it would be hard to imagine anything dumber than making an enemy of the magistrate, which could come back on his House. For decades to come."

I felt my body relax for the first time since Diarmuid had rung the doorbell.

"I hadn't thought about it that way. 'Cause I'm new to politics, I guess. But you're right. I might not've thought that through, but Diarmuid certainly would have before he started down that road."

"Right you are."

"So, then, why would he? Ask her on a date, I mean."

"I guess he really likes her."

"Hmmm."

"I love the way the wreath looks on the front door."

His response was to gather me closer into the sleep

tangle I'd grown to love. His soft rhythmic purring vibrated under the cheek that rested on his pec was a lullaby that eventually put me to sleep.

CHAPTER NINE

Jeremy Irons vs. Gandalf

I WOKE FEELING as anxious as I had before my first court meet. Probably because my little girl was going to be in attendance. All the way to Tregeagle, which admittedly wasn't far, I bent Keir's ear about my concern over Evie and Diarmuid.

"Look at it this way," he said a few minutes before we pulled into the madness that had become the grounds of Tregeagle. Only magic kind would have an outdoor carnival in the middle of winter, since they could choose to be warm in the harshest of environments. "You said she'd had serial boyfriends that you hadn't even known about."

"Uh-huh?"

"And you weren't the worse for wear because of not

knowing."

"I see where you're going but I'm stopping you before you get to the obvious conclusion needlessly. Because there's a giant, gaping fallacy in your argument."

"What's that?"

"I *do* know. And I can't *unknow* what I know."

He sighed. "Well, you've got me there."

Romeo let us out right by the magistrate's private entrance so that we could slip in without drawing a lot of attention. Lochlan was already at work with everything in place and fretting over the fact that someone had sent an urn of flowers big enough to occupy the center lobby of the Waldorf Astoria.

"Anonymous," he said with disgust.

"Why is that bad?" I asked, removing my coat and getting ready to change shoes. "If it's anonymous, it's not a gift that could be viewed as an exchange for a favor."

"That's not necessarily true," he replied.

"Oh?"

He appeared to be mimicking a random person. "Please take into account my sponsorship of the beautiful Yule Court flowers."

"Those flowers were given anonymously."

"The card must've been lost during delivery, but I assure you. They were from me."

I blinked a couple of times. "I see what you mean, Lochlan. The fae *are* a wily lot."

"Keeps you on your toes."

"Recommendation?"

"Toss them out."

"Well."

"Well, what?" Lochlan said.

"It's a have-your-cake and eat-it-too moment. We can make the point and not waste the gorgeous flowers."

AT EXACTLY TEN o'clock, not a second early or late, Hengest went through his impressive ritual to open court while one of his minions slipped a tall cup of my dream coffee concoction onto the bar next to my gavel. Once I was seated, Hengest made the announcement that everyone else was free to do the same.

My eyes drifted over the sea of people to find Evie. Her unusual coppery blonde locks grabbed my eye right away. It also helped that she and Fie were sitting in the front row of the mezzanine. If you weren't in one of the galleries reserved for fae royals and their inner circles, those were the best seats in the house.

She was still a little wide-eyed from the enormity of the spectacle. When I caught her gaze, she shook her head a little and smiled like, "Do you *believe* this?"

Oh, yes. I did believe it.

"Good morning, everyone, and Happy Yuletide," I began. "Before we get started, I want to thank some very generous and anonymous person for sponsoring the awesome arrangement of flowers." I gestured toward the urn sitting off to my left on the dais. "While we can't know who sent them, because accepting such a gift would be frowned upon, the court truly appreciates your thoughtfulness, whoever you may be.

"Now to the business of court meet. Clerk. You're up."

Lochlan rose and kicked us off by announcing the first case. And within minutes the nerves, second thoughts, and doubts that I was the right person for the job had disappeared like the irritating white smoke of a dry wood fire.

Monday was a whirlwind of cases that consisted of minor annoyances and open and shut issues. Among other things, my clerk was masterful at reading the briefs then guessing how much of the court's time would be occupied with this suit or that. He and I agreed it made the most sense to dispense with those that fell into this class on the first day of court week then increase the severity level of grievance as the week played out. Our reasoning was that, if we ever needed to hold over for longer than a week, it would involve only the parties who were directly affected.

Occasionally I noticed Evie staring in Diarmuid's direction, where he was sitting in the House of Bayune gallery. Occasionally I noticed Diarmuid looking her way. It would be hard to say which I hated more.

During lunch break, Evie texted that Fie had taken her out to get lunch at one of the carnival vendors. She said lunch was good. The carnival was insane, the leg warmer/shoe covers looked as white as white could be, and she was trying to get used to the idea of having a mom who's mistress of the universe. I chuckled at that. It could be hard to be humble in the face of that kind of ego-stroking hyperbole, especially when coming from the next generation who, up to that point, had been certain they were the spawn of extraordinary mediocrity.

For the hundredth time in forty-eight hours, I had the thought that I was sorry she wouldn't remember what she'd seen, heard, and shared with me.

ALL IN ALL, I heard twenty-three cases that week. Most didn't even merit a mention in my journal that someday would take up permanent residence in the magistrates' library and become part of fae history. There were, however, four that made the cut and will be written up, technically typed, but you know what I mean. It wasn't that I'm not old enough to be one of the walking anachronisms who still knows how to write in cursive. It was simply that typing was fast and produced consistent, readable text. That would mitigate the ever-present possibility of being misunderstood by some future magistrate.

Tuesday, Lochlan had the day carved into two pieces, more or less, for two cases. Both had aspects that seemed to relate to Evie in totally different, but equally eerie ways.

The first was a case that was of note principally because the argument was compelling and because we'd been unable to find a precedent of any kind.

"Next case, clerk," I said.

"The Welsh lord, Andras Roc-Evans, House of Howland Horn versus the prophet, Hirael."

"The parties will come forward," I said in a voice that sounded comically imperious to me, but by all appearances seemed to carry an air of authority.

Andras Roc-Evans appeared middle aged and might have been thought handsome by some. He had medium brown hair, brown eyes, regular features and wore a costume lifted right out of Henry VIII's court. That included velvet cap with feather, red quilted vest, black cape and a chain of office.

The fae houses seemed to have preferred counsel who'd regularly represent them. Each of these personas was a character I'd found worthy of mention in my journal, partly because I had no doubt they'd still be practicing law before other magistrates who'd follow me.

I believed I was leaving my own stamp on record-keeping as I noted observations regarding their individual tricks, tactics, and tells. Perhaps it had occurred to others and they'd concluded it would be best not to burden a new judge with preconceived ideas about the players. I don't know. I believed that, so long as my notations were as clinically objective as possible, it was a nice addition.

Of course, magic kind who were not affiliated with fae royal courts were forced to tap second-tier legal resources. Unless their cases caught the interest of the Bureau of Behavioral Oversight or, as I was soon to learn, the Office of Freedom for Source Workers.

Both counselors in this case were new to me, which made it all the more interesting.

The man who'd trailed behind Lord Andras Roc-Evans looked like a modern-day English hedge fund manager just stepped out for lunch in the Westminster business district. His blonde hair was clean cut. His blue eyes were piercing, and his square jaw was set with a hint that he believed himself capable of dispatching anyone silly enough to challenge him. His three-piece suit was custom made with subtle vertical stripes and hung on his body with tailored perfection.

The defense table was even more interesting. The defendant, referred to as Hirael, looked like he'd just come from a *Lord of the Rings* Con for which he'd gone to an enormous amount of trouble and expense to look exactly like Gandalf. How I came to suspect that he was the copied rather than the copier was that there was no CGI present in the courtroom to give him the look of a mysterious inner light shining through glassy eyes. He'd defied fashion by going for the mono-color look and was unconcerned that *Vogue* had said it was out that season. Hirael's irises, hair, clothing, and gnarly staff were the same value of dark grey as a storm-rich, cloudy sky. And one might think him penniless were it not for the giant five-inch-high opal set at the crown of said staff.

His counsel looked like a match for Goldman Sachs. I didn't know the name of counsel for the plaintiff, but it seemed like Goldman Sachs fit.

Like Goldman Sachs, the defense counsel would pass for thirty in human years. Being fae meant that actual age was indeterminable. She wore a white silk v neck blouse, with pleats that added softness to the severe look of her own dark, pin striped suit. The hip length jacket was form fitting over a pencil skirt with shin length hem. Her shoes were a highly polished cordovan leather with blocky, sturdy high heels.

She had long dark shiny hair that she wore piled loosely on her head in the Edwardian style most popular with suffragettes. And no makeup other than blood red lipstick. The look was striking. As was she.

When they'd taken their places, I turned to the plaintiff's table.

"Counselor, please introduce yourself and your client."

Goldman Sachs rose, buttoned his jacket, and said, "Yes, Magistrate. I'm Esquire Miles Egress. My client is Lord Andras Roc-Evans, from the House of Howland Horn."

"Very well. Please highlight the facts of the case as you see them, the damages as you see them, and the remedy sought by your client."

"Yes, you honor. At midsummer my client inquired as to whether or not the prophet, Hirael," he looked toward the defendant's table, "had insight into the future of my client's fortune. The man affirmed that he did and said that he would reveal what he knew for a price. An agreement was struck and payment was made.

"Hirael then indicated that Lord Roc-Evans would soon become destitute, that his treasure and vast holdings would be recalled by Queen Arantxa, acting head of the House of Howland Horn. My client believes the so-called prophet is a simple swindler and that no valuable service was rendered in exchange for payment made.

"As to the second part of the court's instruction, Lord Roc-Evans has sustained damages in the form of loss of business and business relationships. Associates who are part of trade or supply heard about the prediction and came to see doing business with my client as a risk. In that way, this became a self-perpetuating prophesy that, if not stopped, would end in the Queen recalling my client's holdings so that they might be managed by someone in a better capacity to demonstrate stewardship.

"Last, my client seeks a return of money paid along with a full, public recantation of his prediction."

"Thank you, Esquire Egress," I said. "You may be seated."

Turning to the defendant's table, I said, "Counselor, please introduce yourself and your client."

She rose to her feet with an inhuman grace that reminded me that, though we share some physical traits, she was without doubt a different species.

"My name is Blythe Merriwether, Your Honor." That simply couldn't be right. This barracuda of a woman could not possibly have a Mary Poppins kind of name. "I'm here on behalf of the Office of Freedom for Source Workers."

"Stop right there, Ms. Meriwether," I said before leaning back to whisper a question to Lochlan. "What's the Office of Freedom for Source Workers? It's a non-profit organization that, among other things, provides legal help to its members. When required."

"What's their purpose?"

"To make sure source workers remain free to practice for payment. There was a time when people who access the Source were captured and forced to use their gifts without recompence."

I nodded and sat up. "Continue, Counselor."

"Very well, Your Honor. Lord Roc-Evans did freely and willingly enter into a contract with my client, made official by his seal and signature. The contract indicates that there's no guarantee that the prophet's vision will be positive or negative, only that it will be the truth as the prophet see it."

"THAT'S FINE PRINT!" The plaintiff shouted from

his chair. "WHO EVER READS THE FINE PRINT?" He looked to the royal galleries as if for support.

"Esquire Egress," I said. "Can you keep your client under control or do we require assistance from the sephalian?"

"No, Your Honor," Egress said. "We apologize for the interruption."

He leaned toward Lord Roc-Evans. The two of them appeared to be engaged in an animated and contentious dialogue, too quiet to be overheard by human ears. At length Roc-Evans gave a single sharp downward jerk of his head, sat back, and looked away from the proceedings as if he'd lost interest.

"Please continue, Ms. Merriwether."

"I was about to introduce my client, the defendant. This is Hirael, a very old and respected prophet with no history of having his work come under question. He cannot recant a prediction he believes to be true. Further, he believes justice would be served with an apology from Lord Roc-Evans."

"Hirael," I said. After taking direction from counsel, he rose to his feet. "Do you work for the Howland Horn often?"

"No more than other houses. I'm freelance."

"How many times have you been sued?"

"Once."

"Very well. Thank you. You may sit down."

To Egress I said, "Esquire Egress, are you aware that your client signed a contract with a clause waiving a particular outcome."

He cleared his throat. "Yes, Magistrate."

"In that case, I'm not sure what we're doing here. That fact wasn't in evidence in the brief or we wouldn't even be hearing the matter."

"I understand, Your Honor," he said. "But while it's true that there is some wording in the contract about no guarantee of particular outcomes, we assert that a belief in general business practice outweighs obscure, easily overlooked legalese."

You had to hand it to him. It was remarkable for a lawyer to refer to a provision in a contract as obscure, easily overlooked legalese.

"Are you saying that there's a general understanding that, if one hire's a prophet, they're going to hear what they want to hear?"

"Well," he said, looking like he was stalling while waiting for the perfect answer to form on his lips, "to an extent yes. There is an expectation of good news."

"I see."

"Well, in the future, people who hire Source Workers will be aware of the pitfalls of relying on preconceived ideas and actually read contracts." I turned to the defendant. "Hirael. I'm not sure whether this will affect your business in the future, but I find for the defendant." I shifted focus to counsel. "Ms. Merriwether, the prophet is not under any obligation to return money or to recant his conclusion about Lord Roc-Evans fortune. Further, your bill will be paid by Lord Roc-Evans."

"WHAT?" The plaintiff was at it again.

I slammed the gavel down. "Along with an additional fine of fifty unimproved hectares for refusing to observe the required decorum of the court after a first warning. And if I'm informed that Ms. Merriwether's organization has to wait longer than a week for payment, the fine will be one hundred hectares." I rose. "Court is adjourned for an hour."

When I reached chambers I noticed that Lochlan wasn't right behind me, like usual.

"Where's Lochlan?" I asked Keir.

"Talking to that woman."

"What woman?"

"The mouthpiece for Gandalf."

I barked out a laugh. "Oh good. I'm not the only one who noticed the resemblance."

"You get the daily double prize for understatement. It was like he walked right off the page."

"Well, what did she want?"

He shrugged. "No idea. But I'm sure we'll find out."

Lochlan entered just as Keir was finishing. "Find out about what?"

"What Ms. Merriwether wanted."

"Oh. This." He held out a note. "She conjured this notecard. Said you'd appreciate the quality of the paper. As she was writing she asked me to give you this. It's a message from Hirael. He was most insistent that you have it, especially in light of your ruling in his favor."

I took the note. She was right. I did appreciate the quality of the paper. I had the feel of heavy cotton, thick and substantial. "You say she 'conjured' this?"

"Yes."

"When you say 'conjured', you mean she like pulled it out of the air?"

"That's right."

"Is she fae?"

"No. She's one of them."

"One of who?"

"Source Workers. Most likely a witch."

"Uh-huh." I could see I still had plenty to learn. "How many subspecies of magic kind are organized in this way?"

He pursed his lips. "A few. Mostly for this very reason. So that they won't be disadvantaged in disputes with rich and powerful fae."

Deciding that I only had an hour for lunch, I let the subject drop, temporarily, and opened the note. In addition to the luxurious paper, Merriwether could teach a class in calligraphy. It read simply, "The virgin will be queen."

"Has Hirael left the building?"

"I don't know," Lochlan said.

"Can you get somebody to find out?"

Lochlan stepped to the door and spoke to one of Hengest's assistants.

"What does it say?" Keir asked.

I didn't answer verbally. I just handed him the note.

He read it. Set it down, and said, "Let's have lunch. We're on a timetable."

"That's all you have to say?"

"Yes. There's little point in addressing a vague statement that could apply to virtually anybody."

I laughed. "You think this could apply to virtually anybody."

"Well, I mean, any, em, virgin."

Hengest rapped on the door with his staff. We knew it was he, because he had a very distinct knock of the triple-threat sort. Loud. Sharp. Startling.

Lochlan opened the door to a young elf with a flushed face.

"He's left the grounds, sir."

Lochlan thanked him and closed the door.

When he turned back to me I was shaking my head in denial.

"No. No. No. No. No. He doesn't get to just drop a

beautiful note card bomb and disappear. I have questions."

Keir took me by the shoulders and said, "Take hold of yourself, Rita. This is one of their games. They pull on a thread of worry in your mind and send it back to you as a prediction so you'll panic, want to hire them, and pay them whatever they want for another morsel of information. No. Don't fall for it."

"It's a scam?"

"Absolutely," Keir said.

I looked at Lochlan for confirmation. "Well…"

"Don't you dare disagree," Keir warned.

"Keir!"

"I need to know the truth here."

"If you bring that crazy old fucker back here, your chance at the truth won't be any better than if you use a Ouija board."

"What makes you think he's a crazy old fucker?"

Keir's eyes widened. "Did you *see* him?"

"I'm not sure I saw the same thing you saw. I mean, he's odd, but take a look at the crowd." My eyes ping-ponged between Keir and Lochlan. "I didn't mean that to sound the way it came out."

Good old Lochlan was quick to want to let me off the hook.

"No offense taken, Magistrate. Magic kind are very much into individual expression. From a human perspective we would seem odd. To be sure."

"What's for lunch?" Keir said.

"Keir. Can you forget about lunch for a minute?"

"No. I'm hungry. If you want to talk about Source Worker carnie schemes, we can do it while we're eating."

"Sorry, Magistrate, but I must agree. We are due back in court in forty-five minutes and would like to arrive with sustenance to carry us through the afternoon."

I exhaled an exasperated huff and said, "Fine, Lochlan. What's for lunch?"

He looked to the table. "Well, let's see."

I love that Molly's pub catered court lunches. She always knew the exact right thing to send. It was uncanny.

He lifted the stainless-steel domes away from the plates already arranged on the table with care.

"I'm guessing the salmon and wild rice is for me," Lochlan said. "The four turkey legs with boiled potatoes and brussels sprouts are for Keir. And it looks like chicken noodle soup with those giant, thick noodles you like."

I did like Molly's chicken noodle soup. As Lochlan said, it was made with big, thick noodles that were yummy and substantial, big pieces of torn chicken breast, cut carrots and lots of green peas. She'd thrown in an individual loaf of black pumpernickel bread and some Irish butter.

On seeing what was waiting for me, I agreed with Keir and Lochlan. There was no reason why I couldn't continue to rant while eating. It was a skill I'd perfected over the years. I sat down without another word and picked up the big spoon provided for my hearty chicken soup.

Keir clapped his hands, rubbed them together, and said, "That's my girl."

I ate in silence, deliberately focused on soup and bread for a couple of minutes, and supposed my clerk and enforcer were too fearful of saying the wrong thing to break the silence.

"Is it true that Source Workers use questionable tactics?"

I didn't say his name but looked at Lochlan for an answer.

He swallowed then said, "Depends on the kind of source worker. If we're talking about seers, meaning those who claim to predict the future, it's the same as in the human world. Such people are sought out for entertainment purposes. It's fun, but not to be taken too seriously. Other disciplines within the general category are less likely to be exploited."

"Why's that?"

"Well, for instance, if a witch is hired for a simple task, say, weed control. It's cut and dried. Either the weeds are still there or they're not. Looking into the future comes with a giant loophole. The seer can always claim that he read the future as it was at the moment he was hired, but since the future is always in motion…"

"And yet Lord Roc-Evans claimed that his commercial interests suffered because associates along his supply chain were influenced by Hirael's prediction of ruin."

"So he says."

"Meaning?"

"That there were rumors about Roc-Evans's questionable business dealings before it got around that Hirael said what he said. It was a convenient hook for Roc-Evans to use as the reason for his losses. And, when a new magistrate has been seated at the bench, some may file lawsuits that wouldn't normally be considered."

"You see?" Keir jumped in, waving a turkey leg like he was making a point with it. "Gandalf probably heard those rumors and used the opportunity to get a fat fee out of a scared Lord. It's exactly what they do."

I looked at Lochlan, who said, "Who's Gandalf?"

"He means Hirael," I said. "Does that seem like a sound explanation to you as well, Lochlan?"

"It does seem highly likely. And I really don't like the fact that he's responded to your ruling in his favor by needlessly worrying you." He stopped and cocked his head. "Come to think of it. Why would that note worry you?"

"Not enough time to explain before lunch break is over, but I will fill you in sometime."

I made peace with my panic. If the two people I trusted most both agreed that the note was bait hoping to reel me in as the next sucker of a mystic charlatan con artist, then I'd take their word for it. And, just like that, I decided to put it out of my mind.

If the twenty-first century had been good for one thing, so far, it had taught us all to be skeptics always vigilant for the next con by email, text, or phone call cleverly disguised as a friendly communique from someone you know, or a demand from a government agency, etc., etc., etc. It seemed that both humans and magic kind are subject to scams devoted to separating people from their money without delivering goods or service of value in exchange.

CHAPTER TEN

Just Jones

The Lady and the Unicorn

LOCHLAN STOOD. "THE House of Guivre versus Rune Lange."

I watched the parties come forward.

First was a long haired, devilishly handsome defendant in a swashbuckling linen shirt, wearing one gold earring. The blonde highlights mingled with light brown hair looked like he employed a masterful colorist and were striking against his tan skin. He veered left and sat down at the defendant's table, Dzbog Bogdan at his side.

Maxfield Pteron, who normally represented cases brought by the Bureau of Behavioral Oversight sat down next to the plaintiff, a petite and stunningly beautiful young woman with dark hair to her waist and neon bright blue eyes. She wore jeans, tucked into knee high black boots and a nubby silk tunic collarless blouse the same color as ripe persimmons.

I addressed the plaintiff first, as was my custom.

"Maxfield Pteron, are you representing the plaintiff?"

He stood. "I am, Your Honor."

"Isn't that unusual? I didn't know you take cases other than those brought by the Bureau."

"This is a case that might be considered a crossover, Your Honor. Had the House of Guivre not brought suit, we very likely would have."

"I see. Well, introduce your client, tell the court the facts of the case as you see them, identify damages as you see them, and let me hear your recommendation for remedy."

"Yes, Your Honor. My client is the Princessa Fayette, cousin to Queen Dames Blanches. The princessa met Rune Lange when she took one of his tours."

Max had stopped and looked at the defendant's table when he named Rune Lange.

"That is Mr. Lange at the defendant's table?" I asked.

"Yes, Your Honor. He owns a fleet of flying vessels

and is known for arranging tours to Asgard."

I've never wanted to utter the word "wow" more in my life, but somehow managed to swallow it and act like I'd heard nothing stun worthy.

"The Princessa and Mr. Lange began seeing each other. Romantically. But eventually Mr. Lange became insistent about consummating the relationship."

"By that you mean the act of copulation."

"Yes, Your Honor."

"Very well. Go on."

"Being physically innocent, my client has enjoyed the rare privilege of the companionship of a unicorn for a very, long time. Acquiescing to Mr. Lange's demand would have meant that the unicorn would vanish and not return. She chose the unicorn. Mr. Lange had a very expensive gem encrusted halter made and gave it to the princessa for her unicorn. The princessa was able to halter the unicorn because he trusted her, but the halter contained a spell to compel the unicorn to do Mr. Lange's bidding.

"That night when the princessa retired, Mr. Lange called the unicorn away.

"The House of Guivre believes it has enjoyed an extended period of prosperity because of the blessing of the unicorn. Queen Dames Blanches and her house want the blessed beast restored to Fayette immediately. They also seek punishment for the caster of the spell that enabled Mr. Lange to steal their most sacred treasure. As for Mr. Lange, we submit a pleading that his license to conduct business anywhere in the territories of the House of Guivre be stripped from him forever more."

I took a deep breath before saying, "Thank you, Counselor."

When Max was seated, I turned to Bogdan and his gorgeous, but very arrogant-looking client.

"Mr. Bogdan."

"Yes, Your Honor," he said as he was getting to his feet.

"You've heard the plaintiff's claim. There's really no need to introduce your client because it was done sufficiently as part of the commentary. Unless you think it would be helpful to add more background, you're welcome to present your defense."

"Thank you, Your Honor. My client, Rune Lange,

dedicated considerable time and treasure to courting the lady with an expectation that the relationship would progress toward an eventual coupling. Mr. Lange's behavior was above reproach. He waited patiently for the princessa to be ready and willing only to learn that she had no intention of giving up her virginity."

When he paused, I spoke directly to Lange. "Mr. Lange. What did you hope to achieve by stealing the princessa's unicorn."

Bogdan gestured for him to stand.

"I thought she would come to her senses, put away childish things and childish ways, and get on with enjoying the fruits of life as a mature female should."

"In essence you thought you would force her to fornicate with you whether that's what she wanted or not."

His face fell. "No. I believed that if I removed the impediment, she'd see things differently. And choose me."

"Where is the unicorn now?"

"In a place unattainable except by one of my vessels."

"And have you consulted experts about the care of unicorns? You know exactly what it needs and when it needs it?"

VICTORIA DANANN

"I don't communicate with it if that's what you mean. Only untouched females can talk to unicorns. But it's fed, watered. You know."

My gaze was drawn to the plaintiff's table as I saw Fayette reach up and wipe a tear away.

"Would you know if it was happy or not?" I asked Lange.

"Happy?" He said the word as if it didn't compute. "It's an *animal!*"

"Sit down," I said.

He did.

"The essence of this case isn't really about whether or not you've taken good care of the unicorn, though you should hope to all you hold holy that you have. The essence is that you stole something that... Well, if I understand this correctly, a unicorn can't be someone's property, but has the freedom to choose whom it spends time with. Is that correct, Max?"

"That is correct, Your Honor."

"And that's why the Bureau is involved in this case?"

"Just so, Your Honor."

"You mentioned earlier that the House Guivre seeks

punishment for the caster of the spell that made it possible for Mr. Lange to kidnap the unicorn. What kind of punishment do you have in mind?"

"A surcharge for services, Your Honor."

"Please explain."

"Henceforth, anyone who chooses to use the services of the spellcaster would be assessed a surcharge of, say, twenty-five percent over market rate. The surcharge would go into the Bureau legal fund. It would also serve as a warning to other spellcasters about using their gifts wisely as a twenty-five percent surcharge is bound to have a negative impact on business."

"I'm sure." Turning to Mr. Lange, I said, "Mr. Lange, who cast the spell for you?"

"Your Honor," he said, after rising, "please understand that it would be ruinous to my reputation to give up the name of an associate who provides a needed service to the community of travel and tour businesses. People would hesitate to do business with me in the future."

"Legitimate businesses whose dealings are above the table would have nothing to fear, Mr. Lange. You're really saying that your reputation with the dregs of your society

VICTORIA DANANN

would be damaged." He seemed to have no answer for that. "It's a clear choice. Tell us who it is or we will confine you until you do."

The man almost gasped. "You wouldn't!"

"Oh yes I would." I glanced at Queen Dame Blanches. "And it just so happens that the queen of French fae was next on my list to perform a service to the court. I have no doubt that she'd be delighted to design the perfect environment in which you could wait while deciding to give the court what's needed to resolve this case."

Lange shot Fayette a look of pure malice before saying, "It was the sorceress, Streghair."

"Thank you," I said. "A wise choice on your part."

"I'll take half an hour in chambers to make my final decision. Court will reconvene at…" I looked at my watch. "Two forty-five."

"All rise," Hengest said.

On the way to my chambers, I was thinking about this court meet had gone so much smoother, all in all, than my first. Perhaps the first time they'd been testing to see how much they could get away with under a new magistrate.

Perhaps word had gotten around that I exact *actual* consequences and not just token fines, which had apparently been the standard set before me and was really no punishment at all.

I sat down at the imposing desk that, more or less, presided over all other furnishings in the room. I tapped my fingernails on the polished surface for a few beats before looking up at Lochlan.

"I'm halfway inclined to give Fayette's mother the privilege of determining the outcome."

Keir laughed.

"Em..." Lochlan said. "You wouldn't though."

"I wouldn't. Why not?"

"Because the princessa's mother might decide that the fairest thing would be burn Streghair alive and castrate Lange."

I chuckled. "Glad we had this talk. I'd forgotten just how psycho fae can be." I looked around, running all the possibilities through my head. "You know Max is really good at summarizing issues, ferreting out actual damages, and suggesting remedies."

Lochlan nodded. "I can't disagree. He's most capable."

"I don't want to get a reputation for rubber stamping what Max says though."

"No. You wouldn't want that."

"Okay. I know what I'm going to do. Visit to the Ladies first."

"Priorities," said Keir.

"Exactly."

WHEN THE SESSION resumed, I turned to Rune Lange. "How soon can you return the unicorn to the Princessa Fayette?"

He stuck out his bottom lip while thinking. It was not an attractive expression. "Nightfall."

"Very well. If the unicorn is returned unharmed by nightfall, the court will be satisfied with revocation of your license to conduct business in French territories. If you don't make that deadline, we will be lifting your most lucrative licenses.

"You can go."

Every eye in the building watched as he stormed up the center aisle and left the building.

I turned to address the plaintiff. "If the unicorn isn't

returned on time, notify the court and additional measures will be imposed. Good luck to you," I added, but a person who has a unicorn as a voluntary resident doesn't really need my good luck wish.

"Bailiff!" I called and Hengest came forward. "Arrange to notify the sorceress Streghair that a twenty-five percent surcharge on payments received will be assessed and collected by the Bureau of Behavioral Oversight. Be sure she understands that assisting clients with magical means to control or manipulate others will, in the future, result in greater penalties."

"Yes, Magistrate," said Hengest.

"Clerk," I said. "Court is adjourned for today."

"WHAT ARE YOU thinking about?" Keir asked on the way home as Romeo hugged a curve with engineering perfection.

"That there were two cases today with themes that are loosely related to Evie. First, the pretty note. Second, the princessa's personal choice to keep her maidenhood for as long as she wanted."

"You could see it that way I suppose. I could also make

a case that it's a stretch to believe those things are related either to each other or to Evie."

"The old I-don't-believe-in-coincidence theory?"

"I don't think it's a coincidence or a sign or anything of the sort. It's like seeing the faces of religious icons in donuts. It's just where your head is right now."

"Hmmm. Maybe," I mused looking out the passenger window into the darkness. "I wouldn't mind getting a tour to Asgard though." As I said it, I was thinking what a marvelous birthday present such a thing would be for Evie. Then I remembered that in another ten days she'd be forgetting all about such things.

"That might be arranged," Keir said.

I chuckled. "Maybe before I ruled against the pirate. Under the circumstances I don't see me getting on board one of his flying ships."

"Vessels," he corrected.

Poseidon's Zoo

THERE WAS A case on Wednesday's docket that I won't soon forget. A merchant-turned-showman had begun capturing specimens of sea life fae for the purpose of a perverse aquarium. His plan was to put them on display for the entertainment of their landlubbing cousins.

These cases, the ones that graphically demonstrate all absence of empathy among some of the fae, were the hardest for me because of their disturbing nature.

As you might guess, the suit was brought by the Bureau of Behavioral Oversight as a template example of what not to do. Maxfield Pteron stood at the plaintiff's table alone but commanded the space and didn't look like he was in need of support. His swagger stick lay on the table in front of him like a weapon at the ready. And for all I knew, maybe it was exactly that.

On the other side was the merchant in question, an Italian named Agosto Mastrioni, represented by Gote Mazza Murelli, who'd made a distinct impression on me by representing another unscrupulous client.

"Max," I said addressing the BOBO representative directly, "let's dispense with some of the needless formality and get right to why we're here. Describe why the Bureau has brought this suit, the damages, and the remedy."

"Yes, Magistrate." He stood. "The defendant has sought to imprison sea life fae and creatures of that world in a sort of club aquarium for the entertainment of air breathing fae. Though our rule in the past has been that fae may do what they wish, most of us honor the more recent tradition of refraining from restricting the independence of others."

"In other words, there's an unwritten code against imprisoning each other?"

"That's one way to put it. This is exactly the sort of thing my organization and this court were created to address. Some of the captured fae have the same level of sentience as ourselves, are fiercely independent, and might be driven mad by incarceration. The complaint is that their freedom was not Mr. Mastrioni's to take."

And who could argue with that?

Max gave Mastrioni a good long look before saying, "The Bureau would like to send a message to all fae that this sort of out-of-bounds activity will not be tolerated. We plead that the court find for us and punish the defendant with the reverse of the confinement he imposed on others."

That really got my attention.

"I can't take into consideration what I don't know,

Max. Spell out for me what you have in mind."

"Your Honor, may I reply by saying that I believe you should see this obscenity personally before ruling. It's my conviction that full understanding can only be gained by experiencing this travesty."

"Where is the facility located?"

"Rome. Of course."

"Of course." I turned aside to Lochlan. "What do you think? Is that feasible?"

"For you to visit the scene of the crime?"

"I suppose that is what I mean. I imagine it's inside faerie?"

"It could be arranged if the Queen Serafina agrees." He rifled through papers. "She was next on the list to do a favor for the court. We can ask her permission and ask her to escort you."

"Do I need escort?"

"You need rapid transportation and Keir doesn't have the necessary permissions to use French airspace."

I blinked a few times. "I didn't know that was regulated."

Lochlan sighed. "Loosely. Yes."

I nodded and sat up. "Thank you, Max. You may be seated."

Turning to the defendant's table, I said, "Mr. Murelli."

"Gote Murelli, if you please, Your Honor."

"Pardon me, Counselor. I'd forgotten your preference for address. Please introduce your client then answer the plaintiff's charge."

"Yes, Your Honor. My client is Agosto Mastrioni. He's a well-known and well-respected merchant from Venice, who now lives and operates his business interests from Roma.

"My client adapted the human custom of putting exotic creatures on display for the entertainment of others, Mr. Mastrioni saw a business opportunity in providing a facility with the usual pleasures plus sea fae on display.

"It's proven to be enormously popular. People, who might not otherwise *ever* have the opportunity to see their oceanic counterparts, come from all over. It's an attraction like no other."

"The greatest show on earth," I said drily.

"Exactly right, Your Honor. We contend that Mr. Mastrioni has done nothing more than exercise skillful and innovative entrepreneurship to provide a unique experience. It might even be thought educational.

"Thank you, Your Honor."

I stopped him in the process of sitting with a question.

"I'd like to hear about the methods used for capture."

"Your Honor…" Murelli began.

"Your Honor, if I may." Max stood to address the court.

"You have additional facts you'd like to add regarding the means of gathering the exhibits?"

"I do, Your Honor."

"Proceed."

"Mastrioni hired a Greek witch to bespell a sonar device with a range of two hundred miles with attraction magic. They discovered on experiment that they could call a particular species by altering the frequency. This combination of fae magic and human magic turned out to be so effective as to render the sea fae helpless to do anything other than respond. They simply swam right into specialized cargo compartments built into ships designed for that purpose."

"Like human legends of sirens."

"Yes, Your Honor."

"How fitting that it was a Greek witch who helped develop the device," I mused. "You said ships?"

"Yes, Your Honor."

"Thank you, Max."

I turned to the defendant and addressed him directly. "Mr. Mastrioni."

Murelli indicated to his client that he should stand. After rising, he said, "I am Mastrioni, Magistrate."

"How many ships did you commission for this purpose?"

"Three."

"I heard Gote Murelli say you're considered to be a very successful merchant." He bowed his head in affirmation. "Still, three ships and crew, plus the cost of outfitting this facility in Rome. What do you call it?"

"Veloce Ionia."

"Uh-huh. This would be an extraordinarily expensive venture even for a rich person."

When Mastrioni hesitated to answer, Murelli stood and said, "Your Honor, may I ask if that was a question?"

"Indeed, you may, Gote Murelli. It wasn't phrased as

such, but is a question, nevertheless. Let me restate." My eyes shifted to Mastrioni. "Did you fund the entire project, or did you have partners? Or investors?"

Mastrioni leaned over and began whispering to Murelli, shaking his head.

"A moment to confer with my client, if you please, Your Honor," Murelli said.

"By all means. Take your time," I said facetiously though I was pretty sure they took me seriously.

After a silent, but furious exchange of whispers, hand gestures, nodding of heads, shaking of heads, Murelli sat down and Mastrioni answered.

"Yes, Your Honor. This endeavor outdistanced even my considerable capital. I do have investors."

"How many?"

"Three."

"And what is their formal designation? Are they partners? Shareholders?"

"Each of the four of us owns twenty-five percent."

"I see." I turned to Max. "Is this of interest to the Bureau of Behavioral Oversight, Counselor?"

Max was agape as he got to his feet. "It is. Certainly,

Your Honor. The Bureau finds that *most* interesting. In fact, would it be possible to petition the court for expansion of the suit to include all parties?"

I smiled. He was quick.

Turning to Lochlan for an aside, I said quietly. "Is there any reason why I could not allow that?"

"It's a most unusual request, but I see nothing preventing you from deciding the issues. You have latitude on this."

"Just what I wanted to hear." I sat up and raised my voice. "Agreed, Counselor."

Gote Murelli was on his feet faster than I would've thought possible. "Your Honor, I protest!"

"So noted," I said. "Sit down."

Though fuming and pink around the edges, he did.

Looking to the Italian gallery, I saw that the queen was in attendance. That was a stroke of luck. I was pleased by the synchronicity of having the Italian queen escort me to Roma faerie.

"Queen Serafina of House Sforza." She stood. "You're invited to be my escort as a favor to the court. And to grant me entrance to faerie in Rome. Do you agree?" She nodded with a proud smile. "Excellent. The court thanks you."

Addressing the court in general, I said, "Here's what we're going to do. Mr. Mastrioni will provide the names of the other three owners to the court clerk."

I leaned over to Lochlan. "How can I get these other three into court this afternoon?"

"Hengest can send messengers with subpoenas." I nodded and sat up straight.

"The court will stand in recess while I take the opportunity to personally visit Veloce Ionia along with my clerk and enforcer. During that time the other owners will be located and served subpoenas requiring their presence in court later today when we reconvene. We'll include sufficient time for lunch for the sake of convenience and continue this proceeding at..." I looked at Lochlan and raised my eyebrows. He wrote two-thirty down and showed it to me. "Two-thirty this afternoon.

"Gote Murelli, I will require that your client accompany the court on this field trip and be available to answer questions."

I raised the gavel and dropped it with a bang.

In the process of getting out of my magistrate's robe and donning my jacket, there was a knock on the door. Lochlan answered and took the note from the bailiff's aide.

"It's for you," Lochlan said as he handed it over.

It was a note quickly scribbled by Evie. It read, "I want to go. Come on, Mom. Please. Please. Please. When will I ever get a chance to visit another world? I promise to love you forever if you'll just do this one little thing for me? Please?"

I chuckled and looked up at Keir. "Evie wants to go."

He shook his head. "She can't. Her constitution hasn't been prepared to withstand the differences in faerie. Yours has partly because you assumed the magistrate's charm when you accepted the office and partly because you've had time for it to reach full efficacy."

"I want to say good. That lets me off the hook."

I quickly wrote, "It isn't up to me or I'd say yes. Your body wouldn't withstand the change. But I will tell you **all** about it. Promise. XOXO."

I HADN'T ASKED what mode of transportation would be used to move me from Tregeagle to Rome. It hadn't seemed important at the time. When the whirring and buzzing of moving so fast through the air, apparently propelled by no power other than the queen's desire, the nausea began. I was prepared to make a prediction that I would not be volunteering to travel by queen often.

"What's wrong?" Keir asked.

I'm certain I looked green. Had I said I was leaving time for lunch?

"Sick at my stomach," I said. "I need a minute."

Serafina turned to one of her courtiers and said, "Bring the guaritrice. Quickly!"

Keir guided me to an ornate bench where I sat and tried to will my tummy to feel okay. It was embarrassing for the magistrate to be compromised by human frailty.

"I thought I got good health as a perk," I said to Lochlan.

He looked perplexed as he gestured toward me. "This must've been an oversight. I suppose we need to arrange for some…"

"Tweaking?" Keir offered, looking and sounding as concerned as if he could understand physical discomfort.

"What sort of aid may I offer while we wait?" Serafina

asked.

"Cool air on my face."

It was no sooner said than done. Cool air was blowing on my face from an unseen source and I felt immediately better. Well enough, in fact to take a look around. It appeared that we were in a grand palace comparable to France's Versailles. The hall was so immense I wasn't sure I could see the end in the distance looking either left or right. It was floored with black and white diagonal marble tiles. The barrel ceiling was forty feet high and painted with murals by masters. The walls were a gallery of hundreds of gold-framed paintings with intermittent candelabra sconces.

It wasn't my dish of tea, but it was beyond impressive.

"Is this it?" I asked, grateful that I wasn't compromising the court by yakking in the queen's hallway.

"No. We're in the outer chamber of the Rome faerie," Keir said.

The bench where I sat was next to immense double doors that seemed to announce that something suitably magical would be found within.

I saw that a young woman was hurrying toward us.

The scarf hem of her black silk dress fluttered against her shins. She was a striking figure with her white hair, black eyes, and blood red lipstick. I didn't blame her for accentuating her lips. They were her best feature, plump, bow shaped, and, I suspected, would look kissable if I rolled that way.

She came directly to me without slowing and put the back of her hand to my forehead like every mother of every child has done at some point, probably since the onset of consciousness in bipeds. She lowered her hand and let it hover over my abdomen while saying a few words I didn't understand. Because they were in Italian.

I was instantly better. You gotta love magic.

"All better?" Serafina asked. Her face expressed a beatific smile in keeping with both her name and station. I was thinking I was witnessing the look of a woman in charge whose authority is never questioned.

Taking a deep breath, I stood and said, "Sorry for the delay."

"Silly to apologize for human frailty," she said. "It is what it is."

"Who can argue with that?"

At that she turned toward the doors. She didn't gesture, or say, "Open Sesame,", or even twitch her nose. Apparently, she was able to gain and grant entrance by pure thought.

The doors didn't open, but rather disappeared so that there was no barrier between us and the scene inside.

"There are many worlds within this mound," Serafina told me. "This is the one that contains the subject of your interest."

Though it was close to mid-day in the human world, it appeared to be nighttime inside faerie. "Is it night all the time?" I asked Keir.

He shook his head. "Oh no. This is a… ah, neighborhood you might say, where it is perpetually dark. You might call it mood control."

"Oh," I said.

The sight that lay before me might best be described as Via Cola di Rienzo meets Las Vegas. In other words, if you were to give the architecture an Italian Renaissance feel, light the pedestrian boulevard with tiny twinkling lights on buildings and in trees, and add tasteful signage, you could imagine the grandeur of the faerie night scene. I gathered that small twinkling lights, normally used for holiday décor, are often called fairy lights because somebody else at some time or another was privileged to witness the fae's elevated notion of clubbing.

The street wasn't crowded but was populated by fae who were openly curious about us. A human, an elf, and a sephalian walked into a bar... Or maybe they were awed by the queen's presence. Or both.

I didn't know how often humans were granted admittance to a faerie mound, but I was sure the number was small and exclusive. It was, no doubt, a great privilege.

I said to Serafina, "It probably won't surprise you that I'm gobsmacked by this."

There was a moment of confusion on her face before she said, "I'm unfamiliar with 'gobsmacked', but if I read your energy correctly, I comprehend your meaning. I believe the appropriate human response to receiving a compliment is thank you."

"It is. Very gracious of Your Highness to indulge my customs."

Looking like a child at Disneyworld for the first time, I tried to drink everything in and lock it into memory so that I could recall the marvelous sights, sounds and heavenly scents whenever I wanted them in the future.

Ahead in a distance that might be compared to a city block, I saw a blue neon sign that was somewhat less tasteful than most. It read Veloce Ionia. Beneath it was a sign, similar to digital animation, showing a mermaid diving into water with tail resurfacing to splash.

"That must be the place," I told Keir, and turned back to see Lochlan's reaction.

Lochlan was stone faced and not giving anything away. Max, however, came forward and said, "Yes, Your Honor. And let me take the opportunity to thank you for the trouble of witnessing this personally before deciding the case."

I gathered that Seraphina was completely neutral about the outcome of this suit. Though it was occurring in faerie, I doubted the existence of Veloce Ionia affected her in any way. She could float above the fray politically, in this case, and remain blissfully ambivalent. Unless, of course, the place was so popular with her subjects as to cause a disruptive reaction if shut down.

We stopped outside the entrance. I could hear faint

strains of music inside.

"So, it's open now," I said.

"It's always open," Max answered.

The queen led the way. The doors opened automatically for her and we followed.

The first thing I noticed about the club interior was the pounding bass beat of club music, similar to what you might find in a human club, and I wondered which society was mirroring the other. Aside from the spectacular, artistic ways they'd constructed the out-of-this-world aquatic exhibition, I noticed that the lighting had blue filters and liquid light patterns that gave the impression we were all underwater.

The "ceiling" above us was a large body of water separated by a transparent barrier that I hoped like hell was secure. These barriers, featured throughout the club were so perfectly clear, without glare or reflection, that one had the impression there was truly nothing separating us from the water.

Above us were countless specimens of mundie sea life, large and small, that swim, crawl, and slither.

The four barriers to water that we might call walls

gave us views of oceanic magic kind. Large octopi in rainbow colors with blinking peacock eyes. Eels with lightning constantly sparking and moving in waves from end to end. Giant pink and coral seahorses with dish-faced horseheads and translucent fins shaped like dragon wings. They were big enough for a normal sized person to ride.

The "floor" below us was likewise a transparent barrier of darker water in which dangerous-looking specimens with very large, pointy teeth swam while appearing to stare at us longingly. The effect of feeling like there was no solid ground beneath me not only made me queasy again but panicked as well.

I grabbed hold of Keir's forearm on one side and Max's sleeve on the other and was gripping for dear life. Seeing this, Keir called the queen.

"The Magistrate is unaccustomed to the architectural interest of the flooring and is made uncomfortable."

Without further discussion, the queen looked at the floor and it became a fabulous example of Roman mosaic tile. She'd thoughtfully complemented the club's décor by using shades of white and blue.

After a few seconds I felt my panic begin to recede and

I was able to release both Keir and Max.

It didn't take long for me to understand why Max had believed I could fully grasp the import of the case by seeing this with my own eyes.

Aside from being surrounded by water, the club has two dozen regularly spaced tubes about six feet in diameter, each featuring a merfae either male or female. These were a most perverse version of dancers in cages.

Though I'd thought I was beyond being surprised that aspects of myths are as real as my cubicle at the insurance company, I was shocked at seeing merfae. I'd *really* thought the notion of mermaids was the ridiculous result of drunken sailors seeing what they wanted to see.

The merfae looked like something out of a fantasy illustration. Mesmerizingly beautiful. Their bodies were covered with scales in shades of turquoise with little hints of pink on the undersides. Below the waist their scales looked thick as armor but got gradually thinner toward the chest and neck until they became transparent, almost invisible. Viewing them up close, as we were at the moment, paper thin and translucent scales could be seen on the sides of their faces.

The tubes were just big enough to allow them to execute a tumble turn. Not enough room to swim and, if the club was open all the time, no privacy. Ever. Fae danced around them as if they were nothing more than inanimate decoration, a feature of ambience, not sentient beings.

They'd been isolated and confined to the equivalent of a human closet, not even as big as a jail cell normally provided for hardened criminals.

Perhaps worst of all, and for me this was inferred by the looks on their faces, they were being tortured by the pounding of bass, which would be four and a half times louder in their inescapable tubes. I passed by four of these. The two males were as still as death. Nothing moved but eyes full of so much hatred that it gave me a feeling of dread as their gaze moved with me. The females looked more frightened than challenging. Both that I passed focused on me immediately and put their hands, with fingers connected by thin pink membrane, on the glass. I can't know what they were trying to communicate, but it felt like pleading for mercy.

I stopped. "Your Highness," I yelled to be heard above the instrumental music.

"Yes, Magistrate?" she turned and raised both eyebrows.

"Has someone used magic to control the amplification of sound inside these containers of water?"

She cocked her head for a second before saying, "No."

"Would it be possible for the court to ask another favor?"

She smiled. "Two plaques?" I nodded. "Could you create silence inside all the containers that hold water?"

"Done," she said.

It was as if the merfae had been held aloft by wires that were cut suddenly and simultaneously. Every one of them immediately sank to the sandy floor of their tube and fell asleep in position reminiscent of sitting. In addition to the torturous assault on their nervous systems, continually sustained for weeks, they'd also been sleep deprived.

Some of the dancers stopped and stared at the sleeping merfae for a few seconds then went back to what they were doing, paying no more attention than that.

"Maxfield Pteron."

"Yes, Magistrate."

"Is there something more you'd like me to witness? Or

have I seen enough?"

"I'm confident that you've seen what I hoped you'd see, Your Honor. I believe the Bureau is ready to rest its case."

I nodded and turned to Seraphina. "Thank you for your assistance on both counts, Your Highness."

She closed her eyes and held them closed for a full second. I took that as a royal fae gesture meaning, "You're welcome."

It was more or less identical to Olivia's show of deference.

After Ilmr guided us back to the human world, I said, "It would be very nice if the court clerk, the enforcer, and I could enjoy lunch in Rome before returning to court. Would that be an imposition?"

"Does that mean three plaques?" The lady was a bargain shopper.

I smiled. "I can't offer that without devaluing the plaques so that they're no longer a symbol of *extraordinary* service to the court. Please return us to Tregeagle."

"Your argument is valid. One of my people will show you to a mundie establishment for a repast suitable to your station. When you are ready, we will return to Tregeagle. We're all eager to hear the conclusion of this episode."

I was temporarily stuck on the phrase 'to your station', but my brain caught up in time to ask, "Um. Episode?"

"I mean to say court case, Magistrate."

I wondered if the use of the word 'episode' revealed more than intended, such as that court meets were reality TV for fae. Oh gods, maybe I *was* Judge Judy!

I managed to say, "I see. That's very kind of you, Your Highness."

Ilmr's strange look caused me to wonder what I'd said. Then I realized that kindness isn't necessarily a virtue from the perspective of royal fae. I hoped it wasn't an insult.

If my goal as magistrate was to alter fae's ideas about being nice to each other, I had my work cut out for me.

We were shown to a private corner of Convivio Trolani where we shared abbachio al forno con patate. Most of the dishes were seafood and I just wasn't in the mood. At all. The tiramisù was the best I'd ever had and went a little way toward restoring my normally buoyant mood.

The queen had left someone at the restaurant who

would notify her when we were ready for a ride back. Unlike Uber, the response was practically instantaneous. A minute later I was standing at the magistrate's private entrance in the rear at Tregeagle.

I looked at my watch. "Fifteen minutes to spare. I'd better get into the judge costume and get ready for Hengest's pounding."

"Hengest's pounding?" Lochlan said.

"Yeah. You know. The way he always pounds on the door like he thinks he's a one-guy SWAT team out on a drug raid?"

Keir chuckled. "He does do that, doesn't he?"

I nodded.

"Perhaps I could suggest that he use a little less force," Lochlan offered.

"Don't make waves, Lochlan. I'm mostly used to it by now."

"You know what you're going to do?" Keir asked.

"Maybe. Lochlan, I've never asked you if I can actually declare something to be a law."

Lochlan raised his chin and I could tell he was thinking it over. "There's no provision nor precedent to give a magistrate that authority. On the other hand, no one has ever tried. If you attempted to proclaim some sort of rule that applied to all of faerie, there might be resistance."

"I know you have a keen political awareness. If you were a pollster, would you think that most of the queens would take my side in a contest?"

He put his third finger to the middle of his forehead, like he was consulting with his 'third eye' or something, then said, "The new system of being recognized for serving the court has been well-received among the queens."

"Have the various houses ever had some sort of joint council?"

"Alliances come and go, but council? Certainly not that included everyone."

I was rearranging the chain of office attached to my wolf medallion when we got the full Hengest-pound treatment. Only this time both Keir and Lochlan turned to me and grinned.

BACK AT THE bench, I was pleased to see that Mastriani's three cohorts stood alongside him at the defendants' table. Good work, Lochlan and Hengest.

"Good afternoon gentlemen," I said, applying the term as loosely as the language allows. "Gote Murelli, are you representing all four partners or just Mr. Mastriani?"

"I have accepted three additional clients, Your Honor."

"Very well. Introduce them to the court, please."

"Yes, Magistrate. This is Count Faschinauct, Mr. Milish Frogsbee, and Jones."

"Just Jones?"

"Yes, Your Honor. He prefers to be known simply as Jones."

Huh. I'd found that the fae love titles and compound names. That made Just Jones an outlier.

"Very well. Have your new clients been familiarized with the case against them brought by the Bureau?" I said abbreviating BOBO.

"Yes. Your Honor."

"Alright. As promised, I have visited Veloce Ionia while the court was at recess and I have some questions that I'd like to direct to your clients. Have them choose which will speak for the four of them."

After a brief discussion among themselves, Gote

Murelli said, "They believe Mr. Mastrioni should speak for the consortium because he is closest to the details of the operation."

I turned my attention to their choice. "Mr. Mastrioni." He stood. "First, how long have the merfae been in captivity?"

"Three months or thereabouts."

"How long has the club been open?"

"Three weeks."

"Do you think of the merfae as being creatures like yourself?"

Mastrioni was definitely confused. "In what way?"

"In the way that you might object to solitary confinement in a glass tube in the middle of a leering crowd with no break, no relief, and incessant jackhammer pounding."

"No, Your Honor. I do not think of myself that way."

"May I ask why not?"

"Because I'm not merfae."

"Do you see any similarities between yourself and the merfae?"

He shook his head and looked bewildered. "No, Your Honor. I do not."

I inhaled deeply. "That aside, let me ask this. At any time between the moment you conceived the idea for this establishment and the present, finished result, did you wonder if your various sea life specimens would thrive?"

"We hired experts to tell us what they should be fed."

"Did you ever wonder if the merfae in particular would be happy in the environment you've provided?"

"Happy?" He looked discombobulated. "No."

"Why not?"

"Because the inner life of fish is not my concern." After a brief pause, he decided to randomly add, "Your Honor."

I looked at the other three. "Would any of you answer differently?"

They looked at each other before shaking their heads in unison.

"Very well. Mr. Mastrioni, you may be seated."

I sat for a brief pause while I gathered my thoughts and stared at nothing. When I'd finally decided on a response, I asked all that's holy to give me the wisdom to say the right thing.

"Before my decision is read into the record, I want to

preface it with some extemporaneous remarks. I'd like to say that I believe the magical community is missing a moral guidepost. In the human world it's expressed in different words, couched in different religious practices, but it amounts to the same thing; what we call the Golden Rule. It means do unto others as you would have them do unto you." For the first time in this court meet, the crowd erupted into a tumultuous symphony of whispers and exchanges that would have been quiet had they not all been talking at once.

I gave it two minutes then struck my gavel.

"Order!" I said, not having any idea if that was a real thing in fae court.

It must've been because quiet was reestablished.

"As I was saying, humans almost universally regard this Golden Rule concept as aspirational. And yet, as one of my fae friends has pointed out to me, for every instance of cruelty and disregard for the feelings of others that I discover in the world of magic kind, a corresponding event in the human world might be cited. That saddens me. Sometimes it sickens me. There may be little I can do about it, but I will do what I can.

"As to this case. The court finds for the plaintiff. Mr. Mastrioni, you will release merfae immediately, along with any of the other creatures who are intelligent enough to know they're in captivity and object to it. And you'd better be sure they're unharmed. As to the marine life that remains, should your abomination of a club remain open, the court will send a qualified inspector who will show up at random times, unexpectedly. His or her job will be to determine whether or not the exhibits in your aquarium are being treated *humanely* according to *my* standards.

"You will turn over the books to an independent auditor of the court's choosing so that we may establish how much money the four of you have made from the wrongs you've done to your aquatic cousins."

"YOUR HONOR!" Murelli was on his feet in an instant. "I object."

"On what grounds?"

"The personal finances of the investors is not part of the lawsuit."

"Overruled. I have made it part of the lawsuit."

There was no mistaking the fact that I hadn't made friends with Gote Murelli, but there's no rule that says a lawyer can't give a judge a dirty look.

"As I was saying, you four gentlemen will pay the Bureau of Behavioral Oversight an amount equal to that figure, as found by audit, to pay for the Bureau's legal expenses." To Max I said, "If there is some amends for the merfae that can be facilitated by money, the court is ordering the Bureau to use the windfall for that purpose."

"Yes, Magistrate." Max was as happy as a crusader can be.

"Further..." I saw the defendants stiffen when I said the word and that was a reasonable reaction because the real boom was about to be lowered. "A special airtight tube with dimensions similar to those in his club shall be constructed for Mr. Mastriani. As a correctional measure and message to the fae community, Mr. Mastriani shall be confined in this tube for a period of seven days and placed in a location popular with merfae."

Again, a din of whispered conversations rose as my ruling sent shockwaves through the crowd. Personally, I thought it was a light sentence. I'd seriously thought about giving him the three weeks he'd subjected the merfae to.

I saw that the color had left Mastriani's face and that

he was staring through glassy eyes.

"Your Honor," said Murelli. "I beg you to reconsider. The man will be ruined!"

"Gote Murelli. Mr. Mastrioni sought to make a fortune from the misery of others. It would be a bridge too far to expect him to be ashamed. But I can make an example of him so that it begins to seep into the collective consciousness that this sort of thing will not be allowed while I'm magistrate.

"Bailiff, please see to it that my instructions are carried out. Court is adjourned till tomorrow morning at ten o'clock."

KEIR HAD SENT word for Olivia to leave dinner, that I would probably want to stay in that night. And he was right. I was grateful to be able to put on my moose slippers and flannel pajama pants and have Guinness beef stew in the kitchen with a pewter tankard of warm red ale.

Evie was rapt while I described what I'd seen in faerie with as much detail as I could recall. When I came to the part about discovering that merfae were real, her eyes went wide. Even my myths scholar thought that one was pure fantasy with no foundation in fact.

"Wow, you're tougher as a judge than you ever were as a mom."

I shook my head. "I suspect that, if you'd enslaved people for profit, I would've done more than ground you."

She nodded. "Point taken. Is it hard?"

"Deciding cases?"

"Yeah."

"It's really not. So far there hasn't been much ambiguity. To me, at least, each case has seemed like there was a clear line between right and wrong."

"Guess that would make it easier."

"Well, guys. Let's let the gremlins clean up. I'm exhausted."

Evie was looking around. "There are gremlins?"

"No." I laughed. "It's just an expression. We used to always say that when you were growing up."

"Yes, but then we didn't think there was any possibility of actual gremlins."

"I'll be more careful with my words. Olivia is a brounie, not a gremlin."

"And there's only one of her," Evie said.

"Unless she brings her brother."

We both laughed.

"I'm going to bed. I don't know if it was the trip to Rome or the horror of coming face to face with somebody who was not only enslaved but being tortured. But I'm too tired to do anything but take a hot, hot bath in my big, beautiful, deep tub then fall into bed face first."

"Must be satisfying though," Evie said thoughtfully. "Your work."

I smiled and nodded. "It has its moments. So does unlimited hot water. Who's babysitting you tomorrow?" I asked Evie.

It's not easy to string three subjects together in three sentences without segue, but shorthand is one of the benefits of conversing with a person who was raised by me.

"I resent that." She pretended offense while I chuckled. "Ivy? I think?"

"Seriously?" I glanced at Keir. "Who's babysitting you while you're babysitting Ivy?"

"Are you saying Ivy's immature?"

"No. Not exactly," I hedged. "Just don't agree to anything she says."

Evie laughed and stuffed the last bite of plowman's bread into her mouth.

LOWERING MYSELF INTO the steamy water an inch at a time, I almost groaned out loud from the sensual pleasure of feeling muscles give way to relaxation. I'm not usually into the whole bathroom-mood-candles thing, but my need for stress-relief was bigger than usual.

Seeing the beautiful merfae trapped in a nightmare may have resulted in psychotrauma for me. Unlike the fae, I have empathy in spades. Maybe to a fault.

So, I lit the candles that had, up to that point, been present for purposes of décor alone. Once it was done, I was so pleased with the ambience that I made a note to self to light candles more often. There was also a small, chest-high gas fireplace, more modern than the rest of the house. I lit it on cold mornings for extra warmth and, almost as an afterthought, turned it on before I climbed into the water. That left the room beautifully lit by firelight. It might've seemed romantic if I wasn't so tired, but my head was not in that space.

With hair piled on my head in a messy bun with chopsticks holding it up and the back of my neck resting comfortably against the curvy rim of the tub, in minutes I was dozing off.

When I heard the door open, I lazily turned my head and opened my eyes a slit. "S'up?" I asked. He began undressing and soon my question was answered. "Oh."

He chuckled as I stared at the evidence of what's up. Keir wasn't the sort to have any inhibitions about me staring at his body. I mean, why would he? He was perfection.

"Got room for me in there?" he asked in the bedroomy voice I loved so much.

"No. You've got your own tub across the hall."

He growled softly, but didn't slow his progress toward the tub. "I don't like that one as well as this one."

"Why not?"

"Because that one doesn't have hot water already run or candles lit."

I laughed in spite of myself. "If that's the only reason, you take this bath. I'll go in there."

He stopped my mock attempt to leave, climbed in behind me, and rearranged my body so that I was leaning back against him. Big, powerful thighs with golden hair flanked me on both sides forming armrests that seemed made to order.

"Still tense?" he said.

"No. I'm relaxed as I can be."

"You sure about that? I might find a way to coax a little more stress out of these muscles that are tight right here."

He put his hands on my deltoids. It didn't take much pressure to reveal that, "Okay. You win. It'll take more than a hot bath to relieve *that* much tension." As his hands began to wander slowly, I said, "How did you know?"

"About what?"

"The stress?"

"I pay attention."

"You mean to me?"

"Why do you sound so surprised?" I didn't have an answer for that. "What's more important to me than you?"

"Um. Sports?"

The hard body against my back rumbled with laughter and I reveled in the vibration of it. "Wouldn't you be surprised if I said yes?"

I twisted my head just far enough to claim a lazy kiss. "I'd be crushed."

What could be sexier than a woman hearing that her man was paying close attention to her needs? Nothing.

I let Keir treat me like a rag doll, rearranging my body as necessary so that he could massage *all* the right places in *all* the best ways. At length when he brought his hands to my deltoids again and pressed, there was no urge to protest. I was as limp as a noodle.

"Come on," he said. "Water's cooling off. Let's take this show on the road."

He helped me out of the tub, wrapped me in my biggest fluffy bath sheet, and did a slow dance in the warm bathroom as he hummed, "As Time Goes By". Me wearing the towel like a sarong. Him naked as the day is long.

"That was the song you were playing the night I found out you can play the piano. It turns out you can sing, too?"

"Just for you."

"Let's go to bed," I said dreamily.

"Thought you'd never ask."

"Who's asking? Consider it a ruling."

"You must be half asleep and dreaming if you think you're the boss of the bedroom."

I giggled. "Well, a judge has gotta try."

Keir finished drying me off, pulled the chopsticks out of my hair and ran his fingers through it like he thought it was the Inca's lost gold. When he met my eyes what I saw there was the promise of going to sleep even happier.

"Light the fire in the bedroom," he purred.

I did.

CHAPTER ELEVEN

Jarls and Jocks

Yuletide Court

TREGEAGLE WAS A happening place the next morning. Word had gotten around that the Norse gods had permitted a lawsuit against the Asgard Council. Such a thing had happened only once before in all the history of Merle the Mathemagician's system. Perhaps I was too ignorant to be more anxious than usual.

Even though it held as many curiosity-seekers as the Kennedy Center, it was packed to standing-room only.

When I was seated, Lochlan's voice rang out. "Now comes the Valkyrie, Sigrid, versus the Asgard Council."

The first person up the aisle was a giant of a man, ruggedly handsome, dressed in a costume of leather, fur, and heavy linen with knotwork embroidery. His hair was long, braided at the temples, and his eyes had a depth that was hypnotic.

Close behind him was the Valkyrie. She wore a simple linen shift, also bordered with an embroidered hem, a fur vest, and boots. She didn't walk but floated just above the ground. Her long white-blonde hair fanned out behind her like a commercial for conditioner, lifted by tiny wings that created a blue like those of a hummingbird. Like the man who advanced first, her eyes seemed to hold a universe of their own, ready for lifetimes of exploration.

The two of them took their places at the plaintiff's table. The defendant's table remained unoccupied.

"Is the defendant in the house?" I asked.

And right on cue, Tregeagle's thick doors opened as if blasted with explosives. What awaited on the other side was the show people had come for.

A man, whose looks and intensity closely matched that of the valkyrie's counsel, sat astride a giant, white warhorse decked out in full battle regalia. It was the mighty power of the horse's front hooves from a reared position that had opened the doors with such unimaginable force.

As he started forward there was no sound and no movement other than that of horse hooves striking the terrazzo floor in the rhythmic, deliberate pace of a slow jog. The air filled with tension, as if everyone present was holding their breath.

When he came to a stop in front of the bench, I thought perhaps I understood literary references to 'being in the presence of a god'. If it's possible for internal organs to quiver, that's what was happening to me on the inside. If was weird. It was scary. It was unnerving.

I waited for him to explain himself.

He didn't.

So, I said, "Are you lost?"

The silence persisted except for a single quiet snort off to my left. Thanks the gods for that familiar snort. Somehow it bolstered my courage.

"No, human. I'm here to represent the Council of Asgard."

"Very well. If you'll have a seat at the defendant's table," I gestured to my right, "I'll invite you to introduce yourself in good time." He blinked. "I'll thank you to address me as Magistrate or Your Honor." I looked at the horse. "And please remove that animal from my court-room."

That sent a wave of murmurs and whispers through the room.

For a second, I thought he might decide to turn around and leave the way he came, but he didn't. He dismounted, said something close to the horse's ear and, to my amazement, the horse turned and walked back up the aisle the way he'd come.

The giant of a man who stood before me turned and gave the Valkyrie and her counsel a good long look then stared at me for another few beats before stomping gracelessly toward the defendant's table. Unlike the other two, this man didn't have eyes with depths that couldn't be plumbed. His eyes seemed to blaze with an internal fire.

Though his features were perfect, there was a cruel set to his mouth and jaw and I strongly suspected I wasn't the only one to see him as a fearsome character.

The way he looked at the chair at the defendant's table reminded me of my first parent-teacher conference when Evie was in kindergarten. The teacher sat in an adult-sized chair while I practically squatted on a chair that would've been more at home in a dollhouse.

I held up my hand. "Just a minute." I turned to Loch-lan. "Who's the next queen on rotation for favors?"

"Queen Ilmr," he answered.

"Fitting," I said, since she was queen of Scandinavian fae. I looked toward the House of Ulfrwulf gallery and saw that she was in attendance. Of course, she wouldn't miss *this* case. "Queen Ilmr." She popped up without hesitation. "Would you be inclined to perform a favor for the court?"

She nodded. "Yes, Magistrate." She quickly made her way forward, stopped to curtsy to the man on the left and again to the man on the right.

Interesting.

When she looked up at me, I said, "The chairs provid-ed aren't adequate for the parties coming before me. Could you be so kind as to make adjustments according to their needs?"

"Of course, Magistrate," she said.

In the blink of an eye the plain bankers' style chairs were replaced by large and comfy-looking leather swivel chairs.

The mean looking giant grunted, plopped down. If

Ilmr had a thank you coming, it would be from me. All she got from him was a glare. On the other hand, the man at the plaintiff's table rewarded her with a gorgeous smile and a nod. She bowed deeply and practically danced back to the Ulfrwulf gallery.

"Very well. Now that we're all comfortable. Let's begin." I looked at the plaintiff's table. Is the plaintiff represented?"

"Yes, Magistrate."

He didn't stand, but I decided not to press formality too hard. I'd make a couple of concessions for gods.

"Please introduce yourself and client, acquaint us with the facts of the case as you see them, outline damages if any, and, if you have a suggestion for resolution, the court will hear it."

"Thank you, Your Honor. I'm known as Forseti. Some call me the god of justice. Some call the god of law. I'm not particular. Either will do. I have on thousands of occasions been in your position, hearing and deciding disputes. This is my first time on this side of the... bar. My client is the Valkyrie, Sigrid. We've known each other for a very long time. I'm representing her free of charge as a token of our friendship.

"The facts of the case are simple and straightforward. Sigrid petitioned the Council of Asgard for the privilege of retiring from service as a Valkyrie. They denied the petition. Though technically there is no higher court, they agreed to allow her to appeal to the fae court and also agreed to abide by your decision."

Yikes! I did not sign up for *this!*

Forseti went on. "As you can imagine, there's not a lot of work retrieving fallen heroes from battlefields these days. Warriors have been replaced with satellite feed espionage and drones. Odin has a place in the scheme of things for warriors who engage in hand-to-hand combat with Iron Age weapons. If the fight doesn't involve swords, spears, axes, or shields, he has no use for the slain fighter."

"I see. First, how shall I address you?"

With a charming smile, he said, "Jarl will do."

"Very good. I'd like to address you client directly if I may." Forseti nodded. "Sigrid, how do you spend your time now?"

"I wait. Mostly," she said.

"For what?"

"The call."

"The call that…"

"The call that tells us… Valkyries that someone suitable for Odin's Hall of Warriors needs a pickup."

I nodded with my whole body feeling *so* far out of my depth.

"How often do you get such a call?"

She shrugged and shook her head. "Never. Anymore. It's just like Fors said." She glanced at him.

"So you spend your time waiting for something that's extremely unlikely to happen."

"That's right," she said.

"Just out of curiosity, and you're not at all required to answer this question, do you have something in mind that you'd like to do instead of, um, wait?"

The Valkyrie's perma-scowl was instantly replaced with a smile that lit up the entire section of the hall.

"I've been breeding fraighounds for fafgaleons and I want to make it a full-time business." Her demeanor changed completely when she grinned and said, "I have pictures of one of the current litters. Would you like to see?"

She held up her cell phone. My day had definitely taken a turn for the better. It so happened that I shared her interest in the future of magical canines and I saw no reason to suppress the smile trying to pull up the corners of my mouth.

"Please approach." I supplemented the direction with a wave of my hand to come forward. "Is this what wolves look like as puppies?" She looked at the screen as if to verify that I was seeing what she intended. "Oh no. Not exactly. These wolves can appear as dogs when they wish. They can travel back and forth between the human world and the magic dimensions. Some of them. These have taken on the guise of Irish wolfhounds."

I glanced at Lochlan over my shoulder with a silent question. He gave a tiny nod. My dogs were the same species as these magical creatures. Wow.

Returning Sigrid's phone, I said, "I can't think of a finer ambition. Thank you for sharing. You may step back."

When she'd returned to her place, I said, "Do you have more to say regarding damages and remedy, Jarl?"

"Yes, Magistrate. We're not petitioning for damages. Only for release of Sigrid's obligation to spend the rest of her days waiting for an event that will not come. It's been a difficult thing to accept, for all of us, that our way of things has passed. But it's time to free those who would forge a new way and leave fruitless obligations behind." He smiled sadly. "In other words, we had a good run. If Sigrid wants to do something more productive, Asgard shouldn't stand in her way.

"I'd like to move for summary judgment in favor of my client, Your Honor."

I took a deep breath. "Motion denied. The court will hear the representative from the Council of Asgard if nothing else as a courtesy in recognition of their agreement to appear."

Looking at the fearsome man sitting alone at the defendant's table, I said, "This is the part, as mentioned earlier, when you tell us who you are."

Without moving from his seated position, he glared at the Jarl, at Sigrid, and last at me.

"I'm Tyr. God of War."

"How shall I address you?"

"Lord Tyr, God of War."

"Very well. Lord Tyr, God of War, thank you for coming. What would you like to say on behalf of the Council?"

With one booted foot he shoved one the banker's chairs away with such power that it careened across the room, under an archway, and crashed into an alcove wall.

In a loud voice, I said, "Where would you like us to send the bill for chair repair?" I said this knowing full well that any one of a number of fae present could fix it easily, including Dolan. I might even take it to the Hallows and sell it as 'the chair kicked by Tyr, himself'.

He didn't answer, but I thought I saw a ghost of a smirk.

"The notion of a Valkyrie doing anything other than what Valkyries do is preposterous."

When he said nothing more, I prompted, "Is that the whole of your argument?"

"No more needs to be said. I'm right." He looked at Forseti. "They're wrong."

"Nothing if not concise," I said. "Might I ask why the idea of Sigrid doing something other than wait is preposterous? In your opinion?"

"Tradition."

"That's it?"

"Yes! That's it! NO MORE NEEDS TO BE SAID," he boomed.

I took a deep breath. "Have you ever seen *Fiddler on the Roof*?"

Tyr scowled. "What?"

"Your Honor?" I heard Sigrid's quieter voice.

Turning my head her way, I said, "Yes? The court recognizes you, Sigrid."

"Let me help dispense with the confusion by saying I'm very certain Lord Tyr has not seen *Fiddler on the Roof*." When she noticed that Forseti was staring at her, she said, "What?"

"You've seen *Fiddler on the Roof*?" Forseti asked.

"Not in person. I mean, I wish I'd seen it in person. Broadway seating is hard to manage with wings. But I've seen the movie like five times. What do you think we do while we're *waiting*?"

"I don't know. I've never thought about what you do while you're waiting. But I know I never pictured you watching... musicals."

"Well, porn gets old real fast."

He cocked his head. "I suppose."

"Excuse me." I banged my gavel. "The two of you can catch up later."

"Yes, Magistrate. Agreed," Forseti acknowledged.

Resuming my talk with the defense, I said, "Lord Tyr, God of War, tradition has its place to be sure, but it's not a powerful enough reason to keep Sigrid from enjoying a full and productive life. Do you have anything more?"

He raised his double-bladed ax. "I have this."

I heard a growl off to my left and felt the kind of fear that precedes the prickly, sick feeling of an adrenaline rush. Keir wasn't created to enforce order in a court with Norse gods as disrupters. I had to stop the momentum toward a confrontation, which it seemed, Tyr would be happy to have.

"The Enforcer will stand down!" I said, looking at Keir.

He wasn't wholly changed but his eyes had changed shape and looked more lion-like.

To Tyr, I said, "That's very impressive. May you wield it in good health and appropriate circumstances. My courtroom is not an appropriate circumstance. As to this case, the court finds for the plaintiff. Sigrid is henceforth relieved of her obligation to Asgard and is free to pursue her own interests."

Tyr rose, yelled at the top of his voice, and brought the ax down with enough power to split the table in half so that it fell in on itself. The horse reappeared at the main entrance, loped up the center aisle and stopped next to his master. Still holding his ax in his right hand, Tyr used his left arm to swing his body astride.

Keir shifted to sephalian form and was clearly not going to take no for an answer.

Tyr turned as if to go, trotted twenty feet up the aisle toward the doors then wheeled to face me. The horse jerked his head and whinnied when he was kicked hard but obeyed and burst into full charge, straight toward me. Fifteen feet before he reached the judge's bench the horse left the ground as if he was going to take flight.

Keir judge the distance and velocity with incredible accuracy and launched himself so that he would intercept horse and rider before I was trampled where I sat. I didn't flight. I didn't fight. I froze and watched sure death aimed at my face.

At the exact moment when the god of war and the sephalian would have clashed in mid-air, Tyr and his charger simply disappeared, and the sephalian landed on the mosaic floor with the soft thud of a thousand pounds on padded feet. He looked around, looked back at me, then satisfied that all was well, resumed the shape of a man. A beautiful, loyal, heroic man.

Yes. I had stars in my eyes, but when Keir took to the air in the face of the Norse god of war it was with full knowledge that he was at a disadvantage. He did that for me. Was someone talking?

"Your Honor?" Forseti was saying.

I shook my head. "Um, yes, Jarl?"

"Please allow me to apologize for Tyr's uncommonly rude behavior."

"That kind of behavior really isn't uncommon for him," Sigrid corrected.

"Be that as it may, we are sorry."

I looked at the ruined table. "Apology accepted. Court is adjourned."

I rose to leave, but Sigrid came flying toward me.

"Thank you, Your Honor. If you'd like one of my puppies…"

I smiled. "You're welcome. I hope you have the most wonderful life. I would take you up on that, but I have two fraighounds of my own."

"You do?" She sounded utterly delighted.

"They're one of the main reasons why life is grand. Be sure they get good homes."

THE FAE HAD come out in droves to see representatives of the Norse pantheon. They came for a show and, I'm sure, they weren't disappointed. In the future, I'd be asking more questions about court cases involving gods. Like, are you sending an all-powerful hothead like Tyr or someone rational like Forseti.

CHAPTER TWELVE

J.D., Again

I BEGAN THIS journal by saying that Lochlan is normally a genius at scheduling, but Sigrid's case took much less time than expected. We concluded the Solstice Court Meet in just four days, which meant I'd gained a day to spend with Evie. Maybe we'd take that day trip to Oxford.

I suggested that very thing over dinner. "It turns out that I've found an extra day. You want to take that trip to Oxford tomorrow?"

Her smile said yes before she got it out. "Yes! I can't wait. What time do you want to leave?"

"First priority is walking the dogs. I'm sure they're feeling neglected. Walking. Eating. We'll go right after breakfast. I can't wait either. I haven't done nearly enough sightseeing. But as time goes on there's less study and prep required for court…"

"It'll be fun. We haven't done a road trip, just the two of us, in years."

"Not since you were in high school deciding which bastion of higher learning would be the lucky winner."

She laughed. "Yeah. And I'm sure I wasn't very good company then."

"Why do you think that?"

I looked at her sideways and we both laughed.

"Honestly though." She looked at Keir like he hung the moon. "When that freaking madman's horse took off into the air and he was headed straight for Mom carrying that ax that he'd just used to chop a table in two that should have required an hour of chainsaw? My heart freaking stopped. I grabbed onto Ivy's arm and squeezed so hard she turned into a pixie."

"She did?" I asked.

"Yeah. It's so weird to be squeezing somebody's forearm one second and have that person disappear the next second. I mean she essentially disappear. She didn't really disappear. She just…"

"Yeah. We know." I chuckled.

"And then Keir." She looked at him. "That thing you turn into. It's hands down the coolest shift ever. And when you jumped up like you were gonna get between that reject from a Viking movie and Mom? Oh my god. My heart really did stop. No joke. If you saw this in a movie, you would not believe it."

"You're not supposed to believe what you see in movies," Keir said.

"Yeah, well. It was so romantic." She nudged him with her shoulder.

He chuckled and put half a fried cod filet in his mouth.

"It was romantic, wasn't it." I added. It was a statement. Not a question.

"Well, yeah!" Evie said. "Every girl wants a hero."

Evie and I looked at each and immediately started singing, "And he's gotta be strong, and he's gotta be fast, and he's gotta be fresh from the fight." That was followed by more laughter compounded by the confused look on Keir's face.

"Keir, my man, I can see your pop culture education is not complete. You're pretty good when it comes to pictures that move, but music? Not so much."

"Hmmm," he grunted good naturedly.

"Can I have a French fry?" I asked.

"No," he said. "And especially no if you don't learn they're called chips and not French fries."

"If I call them chips, can I have one?"

He looked at me seriously while holding the newspaper cone with chips like he was guarding his food. "Maybe."

"Chips."

"Open," he said.

I did, but failed to catch the 'chip' he tossed toward my mouth. "Come on. Can't I get one the regular way?" I wiggled my eyebrows.

"Uh oh," Evie said. "I'm outta here. There are things I do not want to see my mother do."

"Alright. I'm going to satisfy myself with pistachio ice cream and chocolate syrup."

Evie nodded. "That trumps chips any day."

"Right you are."

"Good," Keir said, "I didn't want to give up any more anyway."

"Wow. You'd give your life for me, but not your chips."

He shrugged.

I CALLED MAGGIE to ask if she'd heard what happened in court.

"Are ye havin' me on then?" she asked. "Magic kind in Bolivia have heard what happened in court today."

"Well, this could be stupid or brilliant. I don't know which. But I think we should bring the table that Tyr split into over to the Hallows and sell it as 'the table ruined by Tyr, God of War'."

"'Tis brilliant. No' a doubt about it. We could fetch a pretty penny for such a thing. O' course, we'll need to pay for it."

"Of course. There's also a chair that he crashed into a wall. And two chairs Queen Ilmr created to suit the gods in the house. They're there and nobody's using them. So I say let's pick 'em up and sell them, too."

"Saints Be. Havin' gods come to court is a tidy source of profit."

"Let's don't get used to it. This is only the second time

that's ever happened."

"Oh, aye. Take it as it comes."

"Exactly."

"So, if there's anything I need to know about the shop?"

"All's well."

"In that case I'm taking a day off and going sightseeing with Evie."

"Well, that will be nice for ye."

"Yeah. I'll be by Monday. Thanks, Maggie. Talk soon."

I WILL ALWAYS remember my day trip to Oxford. She was right. She was much better company now that she was grown. I had to admit, albeit grudgingly, that she was an adult. Or close enough.

She fell in love with Oxford while I fell in love with the English countryside all over again.

Did I mention that Romeo *loved* it?

We were back in Hallow Hill in time to meet Keir for supper at the pub.

We told him all about our day then he told us all about helping to move the ruined table and three chairs to the

Hallows.

I played with the dogs in front of the fire for a bit then turned in early.

Loving the sound my silk pajamas made when I slid between linen sheets, I was suddenly bone tired and maybe still sore from the acute tension of thinking my life was about to be ended by a mythic war horse and the god riding him.

When I woke the house was quiet. I sat up far enough to see that Keir, Fen, and Frey were sound asleep. I slipped into my moose slippers and black flannel robe from Harrods and shuffled toward the kitchen without bothering them at all. Suddenly I was gripped by an acute sense of déjà vu. The moment felt eerily familiar.

Sure enough.

Who should be standing in my kitchen, gruesome as you please?

"Yo," said the Jersey Devil.

"Um. Yo," I replied.

"Yeah. So ya don't sound so friendly. I don't blame ya. Last time I promised I was takin' care of business. And, in my business, I don't take promises lightly. Ya know?"

I felt myself nodding even though I didn't know.

"Just thought I'd stop by with apologies and a little somethin'," he said. There was a clink as he placed an enormous horseshoe on the kitchen island. It was some kind of shiny black metal. By the sound of the 'clink', I'd say heavy and one side was encrusted with huge shiny stones that looked like diamonds.

"They're not CZs. They're the real thing. Ice. I wouldn't bring ya a cheap copy."

"Oh," I said. "That's nice. So why are…?"

"Cuz there's still a loose end. Know what I mean?"

"No."

"She's. At. Large."

"The kelpie?"

His chuckle sounded like cement being mixed. "Yeah. The kelpie. Seems she likes it liquid and I…" his wings fanned a little, "don't. But this is not gonna be a problem. I have an associate who's comfortable sleepin' with fishes cause he's okay breathin' underwater. Ugly motherfucker, but gets it done. He's out for this troublemakin' shifter right now. Won't be long.

"Meantime, you can sleep easy."

"Well, that's what I was doing."

"Funny. You make me laugh, Judge."

He wasn't laughing.

"That's nice. Did you bring me something else with no explanation as to why?"

"Things have a way of explainin' themselves in their own good time. Know what I mean?"

"No."

He chuckled again and I shivered involuntarily. "The crystal told you what you gotta know. Right?"

Frustrated, I said, "No! I still have no idea what that's about."

"Now, Judge." He sounded disapproving. "Don't kid a kidder."

"I don't know why you're here."

"A little friendly advice. Stay away from water until I say the coast is clear."

The monster had an encyclopedic range of metaphoric phrases.

"You mean all water?"

"Really. Stop the kiddin' around, Judge. This is serious stuff. We're talkin streams, creeks, rivers, ponds, lakes, oceans, and the like. Got it?

"Stay away from water," I repeated. "Got it."

"Okay then. I'll show myself out."

"How did you show yourself in?"

"You kill me, Judge."

I WOKE TO the smell of blueberry muffins baking. It was Olivia's day off, which could only mean that Keir or Evie was making something yummy. I looked at the clock. It was ten.

TEN! Good Glory. I hadn't slept until ten since the last time I'd had a procedure that required anesthesia.

Keir was pulling gorgeous giant blueberry muffins with perfect golden-brown tops out of the oven.

"Where's Evie?" I asked, tying the belt of my robe.

"Didn't you say she had a date with Diarmuid?"

"Oh yeah. I forgot."

When the doorbell rang, Keir started wiping his hands on the half apron tied at his waist.

"I'll get it," I said as I was opening the door.

"Mornin' Magistrate," Diarmuid said with a smooth smile. "'Twas an excitin' day at Tregeagle yesterday."

Nodding, I said, "It was."

"I went to the cottage to call for Evangeline, but she's no' there. Is she here?"

He was looking over my head like he needed to see for himself.

"No."

I heard Keir behind me. "We thought she was with you."

Diarmuid scowled. "Where did she say she was goin'?"

Keir sighed. "Let him in. Come into the kitchen. I have muffins."

When the three of us arrived in the kitchen, Keir put the blueberry muffins on the island and turned to Diarmuid.

"I told her I saw you leaving the guesthouse. I knew it would worry her mother if she knew the two of you were sneaking about. Evie got mad and said she was going for a walk."

After giving Diarmuid a seriously long, accusing look, I asked Keir, "How long ago was that?"

"Couple of hours."

"Did she no' say anythin' about where she'd be

walkin'? I mean, she knew we had plans."

Diarmuid cast his eyes about the kitchen like he was looking for clues. His gaze landed on the horseshoe. "By the gods, how did you get this?" He snatched it up. "'Tis mine."

"What do you mean it's yours?" I asked.

"Belongs to one of the horses that pull my chariot when…"

Keir and I exchanged a look.

"Wild Hunt?" I asked.

"Aye." Diarmuid turned it over and over, clearly mystified as to how it might have ended up here in my kitchen.

"It was a gift from a nocturnal visitor."

Keir gave me an odd look. "The same one that left the crystal?"

"The very same," I said.

"She said something about it being a good time to get out and see the mill house that everybody's always talking about. She's probably down by the river and lost track of time."

I felt my stomach fall like I was in a too-fast elevator

while a cold fear closed my throat and stole my words away.

Stay away from the water.

PREVIEW BOOK THREE

Midlife at Midnight

Beltane at Hallow Hill

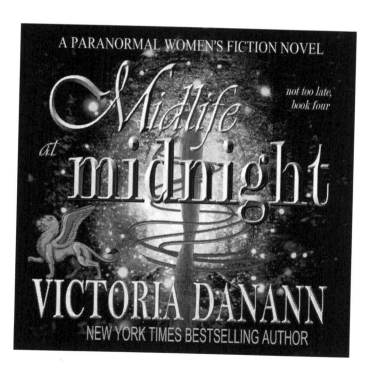

EVIE IS MISSING!

Rita is hysterical. Keir is near panic. Diarmuid is beside himself.

The thrilling tale of the Wild Hunt as a first responder rescue unit.

And a Beltane Handfasting like no other.

Victoria Danann®

NEW YORK TIMES and USA TODAY BESTSELLING AUTHOR

Victoria's Website

victoriadanann.com

Victoria's Facebook Page

facebook.com/victoriadanannbooks

I know you get hounded for reviews for everything from sunscreen to refrigerators. I feel your pain. But reviews are enormously helpful to me personally. Please take a second and rate this book.

ALSO BY VICTORIA DANANN

PARANORMAL WOMEN'S FICTION (for all the *everyday* heroines over forty)

Not Too Late 1. **Midlife Magic**

Not Too Late 2. **Midlife Mayhem**

Not Too Late 3. **Midlife Mojo**

Not Too Late 4. **Midlife at Midnight**

Not Too Late 5. **Midlife at Midsummer** (a novella)

THE KNIGHTS OF BLACK SWAN

Knights of Black Swan 1. My Familiar Stranger

Knights of Black Swan 2. The Witch's Dream

Knights of Black Swan 3. A Summoner's Tale

Knights of Black Swan 4. Moonlight

Knights of Black Swan 5. Gathering Storm

Knights of Black Swan 6. A Tale of Two Kingdoms

Knights of Black Swan 7. Solomon's Sieve

Knights of Black Swan 8. Vampire Hunter

Knights of Black Swan 9. Journey Man

Knights of Black Swan 10. Falcon

Knights of Black Swan 11. Jax

Knights of Black Swan 12. Trespass

Knights of Black Swan 13. Irish War Cry

Knights of Black Swan 14. Deliverance

Knights of Black Swan 15. Black Dog

Knights of Black Swan 16. The Music Demon

*Order of the Black Swan Novels

Black Swan Novel, Prince of Demons

THE HYBRIDS

Exiled 1. CARNAL

Exiled 2. CRAVE

Exiled 3. CHARMING

THE WEREWOLVES

New Scotia Pack 1, Shield Wolf:

New Scotia Pack 2. Wolf Lover:

New Scotia Pack 3. Fire Wolf:

WITCHES and WARLOCKS

Witches of Wimberley 1. Willem

Witches of Wimberley 2. Witch Wants Forever

Witches of Wimberley 3. Wednesday

CONTEMPORARY ROMANCE

SSMC Austin, TX, Book 1. Two Princes

SSMC Austin, TX, Book 2. The Biker's Brother

SSMC Austin, TX, Book 3. Nomad

SSMC Austin, TX, Book 4. Devil's Marker

SSMC Austin, TX, Book 5. Roadhouse

Cajun Devils, Book 1. Batiste

Made in the USA
Monee, IL
05 June 2021

70334094R00210